INTO THE WEST

INTO THE WEST

SAN JUAN WRITERS

GLORIA O'SHIELDS, EDITOR

Printed in the USA

San Juan Writers is located in Farmington, New Mexico.
This project funded in part by the Connie Gotsch Arts Foundation. ^G

ISBN: 9781086568875

Saddle your dreams afore you ride 'em.
—Mary Webb, English Novelist 1881-1927

CONTENTS

FOREWORD

The members of San Juan Writers have done themselves proud with this collection of their respective works. It is a delightfully eclectic collection of fourteen short fiction items which range from tales of the old west to fantastic tales of days that never were. There is a tale of a barroom gunfight in one entry and a shootout with bank robbers in another. Those two are juxtaposed with an account of an attack by inbred turkeys and another which features a war between giant owls and ancient spirits with injury to the humble humans who happen to get in the way. There is a tale of fulfillment of an ancient Native American prophesy. Some of the stories are lighthearted and offer a chuckle while others border on the noir and end with a tragic gasp. They share originality and competent, well-written, presentation. That is to say, there is never a dull moment on any page in this little collection. I look forward to seeing San Juan Writers' next anthology.

Don Bullis
New Mexico Centennial Author

ACKNOWLEDGEMENTS

Each member of San Juan Writers contributed their skill, imagination and creativity to produce the works of fiction included in this volume. Yet, SJW could not have put together a project like *Into the West* without the assistance of others. The supportive people recognized here were essential to the successful completion of this collection.

This project was funded in part by the Connie Gotsch Arts Foundation. We are extraordinarily grateful to the foundation for having faith in this endeavor.

The Foreword for this book was contributed by Don Bullis, noted New Mexico historian and New Mexico Centennial Author. We sincerely thank him for his assistance and kind words.

What is a book without a cover? Our gratitude goes to DelSheree Gladden for the wonderful cover layout and to Vicky Ramakka for providing her beautiful photograph of one of New Mexico's fantastic sunset.

We are indebted to the following authors for reviewing our manuscript and providing their impressions of the collection: western writer Jim Griffin, novelist and memoir author Tekla Dennison Miller, New Mexico mystery writer Margaret Tessler, and as previously mentioned Don Bullis.

Every group needs a place to meet and work. We offer special thanks to Bethany Christian Church in Farmington, New Mexico, for their generosity over the years in providing a room for our meetings.

Most important of all, we thank our families for their love, support, and indulging our enthusiasm for this anthology.

INTRODUCTION

Into the West is a collection of short stories and a novelette written by members of San Juan Writers. In this wide-ranging collection of unique tales you will encounter mystery, adventure, romance, humor, horror, and magical realism. All the stories are set in the American West—some tell of the past while others reflect today's themes.

San Juan Writers was formed in 2002 by a small group of New Mexicans with the goal of helping one another master the craft of writing publishable manuscripts. Today we are eight writers strong who meet weekly to critique each other's works-in-progress. With support from SJW, our members have previously published novels, short stories, poetry, and works of nonfiction.

A brief biography of each contributor is included at the end of this collection to give you chance to learn more about our talented writers.

Journey with us, *Into the West.*

Gloria O'Shields
Editor

UNINTENDED CONSEQUENCES —TERRORIST TURKEYS

Vicky Ramakka

*T*he *Farmington, New Mexico, Daily Times newspaper carried a story on March 19 headlined, "A Case of Troublesome Turkeys." Seems the Westland Park neighborhood was in a tizzy about wild turkeys. Some folks were claiming turkeys living in the nearby woods were harassing children and causing havoc to their property. A follow-up article related that wildlife department officials planned to relocate the offending birds.*

Such tampering with nature could have unintended consequences. This led to speculation about just where this practice might lead. Let's project into the future—say three years from now...

Reports on human-animal conflicts skyrocketed as neighborhoods spread into former wildlife habitat. Like other wildlife agencies across the west, the New Mexico Wildlife Department began relocating nuisance wildlife as standard practice. As they rounded up troublesome turkeys, Conservation Officers explained to onlookers that

1

delinquent birds are transported to remote areas and released in habitat more suitable for the wild creatures. In New Mexico, the designated release site was between Navajo Lake and the Carson National Forest. The miscalculation was that no one anticipated freeing all miscreant birds in one place would spike the gene pool.

At first, it was only stories from hikers who ventured deep into the backcountry. Tales surfaced about gangs of tom turkeys in full strut, chests puffed out and tail feathers flared, challenging peoples' right to pass on hiking trails. Rumors spread about flocks of turkeys swarming through camps at night—overturning coolers, pecking holes in tents, yanking guy ropes loose. Of course, the biologists explained, tom turkeys *are* aggressive in the spring, and a bunch of big birds do make a mess when they pass through. Even with these biological insights, word went out among recreationists, "Stay out of the Carson."

Next it was the hunters. Some reported an eerie feeling that they were being watched. But when they swung around ready to aim, there was nothing except the sound of cackling just out of range. The camp destruction continued. Raids now took place during the day, after hunters had left camp. The terrorists had adapted their tactics.

Not only pillaging, but downright viciousness occurred. One elderly hunter had brought along his companion cocker spaniel. Little Ruffy always stayed in camp and never made any trouble. One evening, as the hunters returned to camp, they cursed the wreckage that lay before them. They thought Little Ruffy, backed up against the tent, was just embarrassed that he had let them down as camp guardian. When he finally stood up to greet his master, the last of the group to return, they were astonished to see that every hair had been plucked from Ruffy's tail.

Except for the local Quick Stop and Bait Shop selling fewer sandwiches and six-packs, there was little noticeable economic impact. That is, until the day Bud Woods, owner of the largest timber company in Rio Arriba County, arrived at the Carson National Forest headquarters to complain that somebody had to do something about those turkeys. Madera Timber Company had won the bid to harvest 160 acres of second growth. The company had completed the paperwork, cooperated on studies, and tolerated the Tree Hugger protests. Now, he demanded, there had to be some assurance that his people could work without harassment.

The Forest Supervisor never cracked a smile as Mr. Woods outlined the attacks. Initially, they thought the hits were random occurrences. But the previous week, for two days in a row, a pair of surveyors came out of the woods roughed up, bleeding and scared. They kept repeating, "They hit us out of nowhere." The two toughest Madera Timber Company surveyors refused to set foot in the forest.

Next it was their chief forester, who was out marking which trees were to be cut. He got it the worst. Members of the search party reported that it took them an hour to talk the victim down from the tree. They weren't sure whether it was because he was just plain scared or because he had been stripped naked.

The man's left Red Wing boot was found 37 feet from the right one. His suspenders lay stretched across the ground, as if they had been, well, played with—pulled out and released again and again. The sleeve of his red Woolrich shirt hung over a limb 10 feet off the ground, almost like a victory flag.

The Company sent out word that no employee was to work solo on the Carson National Forest. "GO ONLY IN TEAMS," the memo warned. But that wasn't enough. Bud Woods demanded protection for his men. He wanted permission for armed guards to accompany every logging crew, and he wanted the government to pay for them. It wasn't his fault those *@!* turkeys got so mean.

The Forest Supervisor related that wildlife, especially nuisance wildlife, came under the purview of the New Mexico Wildlife Department. He would contact the Wildlife Department immediately. Bud muttered that the situation was way beyond the nuisance stage and stomped out.

The Wildlife Department recognized the problem but considered the whole thing a local anomaly. They never wavered from the capture and release program. It was written into their Plan, documented by

3

expert biological opinion, and highly endorsed by the public relations officer. After all, the capturing of miscreant turkeys rummaging among garbage cans or terrifying cats caused commotion enough, without the outdated practice of wringing their necks while the neighbors watched. So, into cages they went for a scenic ride to Carson National Forest.

It was about the tenth capture when the Conservation Officers pulled into the clearing where they always released offending turkeys and noticed the surly-looking gobblers standing guard. The sightings got to be routine. By the eighteenth release, the Officers found themselves nervously dumping their cargo and speeding back to the main road. It was obvious those toms had become super-Alpha-turkeys. They were waiting to initiate the newcomers into their feathered brotherhood.

Maybe if the Conservation Officers had reported the intimidation behavior emerging at the release site, it would have made the Wildlife Department re-examine its turkey relocation program. But how could the Officers admit that ill-tempered turkeys were causing them to reconsider their career choice.

Nothing really happened until the Governor's visit. The Four Corners Boy Scouts decided to hold a dedication ceremony at their campsite near the forest. Refuting the image of the "sit-behind-the-desk bureaucrat," the Governor was well known for a penchant for publicity. So, no one was surprised that the Gov accepted the invitation to cut the ribbon for the Troop's ceremony.

The event was widely publicized. Still, nobody knew exactly how word got to the turkeys.

Up at the campsite, the ceremony itself went fine. Lots of dignitaries, uplifting speeches, Boy Scout badges glinting in the sunlight, firm handshakes all around. It wasn't until everybody returned to their vehicles that the attack became obvious—both visually and olfactorily. Every car, every SUV, had been bombarded. Even the unmistakable Wildlife Department green trucks were WHITE.

This was intolerable. This was the last straw. All eyes turned to the lone Wildlife Department representative. Scarlet faced, but with

4

notable graciousness, she grasped the squishy handle of each and every door, allowing the dignitaries to maneuver themselves into their vehicles with utmost care *not to touch anything*.

No longer were the news reports humorous. They were vitriolic. *"Terrorist Turkeys Attack." "Governor Bombarded." "Somebody Fooled With Mother Nature."*

The lights burned late that night at Wildlife Department headquarters in the state capitol. When the phone rang just seconds after the 10:00 p.m. news broadcast, they knew it would be the Governor. "WHAT are you people doing? Dumping dysfunctional turkeys from the whole state in the same area? You've created a race of super aggressors. Do something!" It was a short conversation.

As the Director hung up the phone, the solution hit him right between the eyes. This problem started with genetics, it had to be fought with genetics. Thus, word went out to field personnel throughout New Mexico. Immediately capture and transplant to the Carson National Forest, any turkey observed committing random acts of kindness.

A SPIRITUAL REBIRTH

Anthony Bartley

It started that night in early fall, 1910, when I came home to a bloody mess in the kitchen.

The oil lamps were unlit, and a murkiness fell heavy on the room. The coppery stench of slaughter permeated the air. I ran to my wife Sarah's side and knelt by her half-naked body, ignoring the pool of blood congealing around her legs. My first thoughts were someone had broken in then defiled and injured her. That's been known to happen out here in the backwoods of Colorado. I scooped her head into my hand and wiped away her black sweat-matted hair with the other.

"Honey, what the hell happened here?"

A moan answered. Her eyes opened as if the lids were weighted down. I felt her hand brush by my thigh then fall onto the floor.

"Sarah, I have to get you into town, to the doc—" I started, but her scream cut me off.

"No David! No! I'm okay, but the baby..."

The baby? What about it? It was due at any time. Although there was a lingering paunch, her stomach was noticeably smaller. The shock of seeing her lying in a gory pool had washed away all thoughts of her pregnancy. My stomach now lurched with fear. I looked around for the infant but saw nothing but a dribbled trail of blood that started from Sarah, went past the cast iron stove, and down the cellar steps. I gazed at the cellar then back to my wife. I heard nothing that indicated a living child.

"Sarah, what happened?" I stroked her pale cheeks.

"It came so quickly. I didn't have time to—" She sobbed.

I attempted to quiet and soothe her, but to no avail.

"Can you get up, honey? I need to get you to a doctor."

"No, we can't go to him. He'll know."

"Of course he will know. He'll understand."

She pleaded with teary eyes and struggled to stand up. I grabbed a chair and helped her into it. As she sat, I became increasingly distressed at the silence and the lack of an infant. I headed toward the open cellar door. Sarah wailed and reached for me.

"I have to check, Sarah. I just have to."

Her moans followed me down the steps.

The darkness in the small room swallowed my vision. The dank smell of earth and blood pervaded the scene. Shuffling through the gloom, I stumbled over a coil of rope used for clothes lines. I found a match in my pocket and lit it. Heat crept close to my fingertips as I carried the small flame and touched it to the wick of an oil lamp.

When the light flickered the darkness away, my heart plummeted into a well of despair. A stained dishtowel covered most of the baby. Only its tiny, pale hand protruded from the edge of the cotton shroud. The meaty afterbirth lay above the newborn's head. My wife's undergarments were in a pile nearby.

I crept over to the small figure on the floor and knelt.

Snakes squirmed around my brain as I reached with a trembling hand and pulled away the covering. The towel stuck to dried fluids on the body. I felt frightened, disgusted, and horrified at the circumstances

7

to which I had come home. Upstairs, I heard Sarah sobbing and sniffling.

A frail baby girl lay exposed on the earthen floor. Grains of dirt clung to her bluish-gray skin. A few ants had found her. I brushed them away. A tiny tongue protruded from her mouth, but her eyes were closed. Her limbs splayed wide as if waiting to be picked up from the cold ground. Stretching from the naval and wound tight around her neck was the umbilical cord.

"David?"

I jumped from the close voice and the hand that touched my shoulder. Puffy eyes gazed into mine when I turned. Sarah trembled violently. Her hair was a disheveled mess.

She squeezed my shoulder and looked away from me. "They'll know, David. Everyone will know, I…" She swallowed, "had a baby."

I stood, grasped her chin, and turned her head. "Sarah." I tried to think what I might say to ease her. "This type of thing happens. They won't blame you. I promise." I watched her brown eyes shift from fright to pleading again.

Her lower lip quivered. "They will blame me, David." She gripped my shirt with talon-like fingers. "Everyone *will* say it's my fault."

"Sweetheart, they will understand." I paused to compose myself. "If anyone is to be blamed, they'll blame me. I should have been here."

Sarah only stared at me. A grimace contorted her fine features. As suddenly as it had come, the pain in her face dissipated. She smoothed down her blood-smeared blouse. "I have to clean up." She turned and walked away. Without stopping, she said, "I don't want anyone to find out, David. Please, find her a good place." My wife hobbled up the stairs, leaving me with the small, cold corpse.

*****

I guided the horse cart a short distance to a place I always considered pretty. It was a piece of land with aspen and pine trees. High sandstone cliffs jutted up and ran parallel to the road. Oak brush and bluegrass sprouted among the rocks and trees.

A three-strand barbwire fence nailed to cedar posts separated the property from the road. I parked the cart and set the brake. Reaching over the seat, I lifted the blanket-wrapped baby. I still recall her infant weight and form in my hands. Nausea, sadness, anger, shock, all tumbled around in me. Stepping onto the packed dirt of the road, I realized I left my lantern hanging on the front porch. A three-quarter moon provided adequate light. I slipped between the barbwire strands.

With shovel and mattock under my right arm and my dead child held in the left, I trekked out to the burial spot. Underlying the pleasant scent of pines and wet grass, an odor of dried blood crawled in to assault any possible comfort. I only had to walk a few yards onto the property before finding a thick, white-barked aspen. The tools fell from my arm. I placed the bundled blanket on a full oak bush. The branches sagged but held the baby. I retrieved the mattock. Under the aspen tree, I dug. Breaking through roots and rocks, I dug.

Though the night was cool, sweat trickled down the side of my face and soaked through my shirt. My hands were raw and achy from the chopping and shoveling. I stood and massaged my lower back. A breeze blew across my damp skin, soothing my flesh. The leaves and pine needles whispered their secrets to one another while an oak bush held mine.

I gathered the bundle from the branches. Placing her upon the ground, I opened the blanket and stared at the tiny figure. I unwound the stiffened umbilical cord from her neck then took a canteen of water from my belt. A damp handkerchief wiped my baby clean. I swallowed what water was left but struggled to keep it down. The grave was only three feet deep but sufficient to hold my child.

With the infant in her earthen crib, I gathered pine branches and laid them upon the bundle in the hole. I didn't want scavenging coyotes to dig her up and hoped that the pine scent might mask the odor of a decomposing body. I shoveled dirt into the hole, found several large rocks and set them upon the grave. Taking out my pocketknife, I carved "Mary" into the white bark.

*****

Three weeks passed. I thought Sarah might be able to get herself back into regular life, but she couldn't. She was always a little odd—thinking visitors were coming to get her or hearing whispers when we were alone. Things worsened after she was with child, and worse still following the birth. She became fanatical in her religious faith and meticulous about housecleaning. We were never strict church-going folk, but I followed her to the services on occasion. Whenever she could, Sarah read the Good Book to me, but listening was the extent of my devotion.

When she started hearing baby sounds, my mind twinged with dread for my wife.

I remember the night she woke me up by repeatedly slapping my face in panic. "David. David. Wake up! Do you hear it?" she said in a desperate whisper.

I grabbed her hand to stop the pain in my left cheek and sat up.

"Do you hear?"

I listened, thinking we had an intruder, but heard nothing except the whooshing within my own ears. "No." I smelled her fear, sour and musky.

Sarah clutched my arm, digging her nails into the flesh. The pain magnified in my hazy state. I winced. My cheek throbbed from the earlier pummeling. She stopped moving, seeming to focus on listening.

"I don't hear anything."

Sarah squeezed again to quiet me. "A baby, David. I—I hear a baby *cooing*."

I peeled my darling's hand off and pulled her to me. "No, honey. There's nothing. It's just another one of your nightmares." I rocked her back and forth, trying to slow her shivering. I knew her eyes remained wide open, probing the dark corners of the room.

*****

Sarah awoke every night to the baby noises. Her mental scars ran deep. I hoped I could be a pillar in her life and draw her out of the madness. My love for her shattered my reasoning and blinded my mind to the truth. The ghost sounds became worse. She heard not only cooing

10

but also crying, and not just at night but all hours of the day. Sometimes, she became so convinced that I thought I heard them, too.

*****

With our nearest neighbor a mile and a half away, we kept to ourselves. It was difficult not socializing with anyone but my troubled wife. Now, even more distressing than her fits, was that *I* saw things. Baby-type things.

While brushing my old mare Milly one evening, I noticed her eyes grow wide. She stomped, reared her head, and backed out of the stall.

"Ho, girl!" I grabbed her halter. "What's got into you?"

She tugged from me, staring at the loose straw in front of her pen. I followed her gaze. Something moved within the flaxen pile. A sharp snorting from behind startled me. I turned and rubbed Milly's soft, fleshy nose.

"Lord Amighty, horse. Why you getting yourself all worked up over a mouse?"

She pawed the ground.

I reached over the stall and retrieved the pitchfork to get rid of the annoyance. I turned to jab the tines into the fodder but shock stayed my thrust. A miniature fist pushed through the straw. The hand opened and strained as if reaching for me. I saw a lump wriggle beneath the rough, golden blanket of hay.

"What in God's green earth? How?"

My fingers ached from gripping the fork handle. My arms shook. I released the pitchfork and dropped to my knees. Slowly, I picked up a handful of straw. There she lay, staring at me like a blessed little angel. I reached down to gather up my child, my Mary.

As I placed my hands on the babe, her face turned gray and bloated. Her eyes and tongue bulged. Her baby hands quivered then fell. She dissolved like snow before a burning sun until all that remained was a shallow indentation in the straw.

My body trembled, and a squealing sob made me look up, only to realize it had come from me. I cupped my face with both hands and wept. I worked to rub the image from my eyes. My heart felt as though someone had wedged a hammer claw behind it and tried prying it out of my chest. Old Milly's nibbling on my hair snapped me out of the ghastly vision.

I stood and leaned on the horse, smelling her animal fragrance. The baby's dying face was all that passed through my mind. Could my wife's insanity be contagious?

*****

Two months had passed since Mary's birth. I often wondered what happened that night. While I cut the firewood, my mind turned over memories of the nightmarish vision. With each push and pull of the saw blade through the log, a new terrifying image of Mary dug into my mind like the saw teeth biting into the timber. I needed to visit her grave to find some respite in this madness. Maybe seeing her name, talking to her would bring solace.

That afternoon, I picked a small bouquet of daisies and wild baby's breath for the grave. The name, Mary, carved into the white bark had become dark and scabby. Placing the flowers on the stones, I noted that everything seemed as it should—no digging, no disturbance of any kind around the gravesite.

"I'm sorry." My eyelids burned with tears as I knelt and patted the center stone. "You didn't even have a chance to take your first breath. If only I'd been there you might be with us today, but there's nothing to be done now, is there?" Guilt cracked my heart and sorrow seeped from the wounds.

The scent of blossoming honeysuckle and dry earth eased the memories of when last I was there. Aspen leaves shimmered in the wind and reflected sunlight.

Holding it in no longer, choking sobs wracked my body. I cried for a long while.

*****

When I arrived home, the pleasant aroma of dinner cooking filled our small kitchen; a smell that had been absent for many months.

12

Sarah diced an onion to place into a frying pan full of potatoes. A roast sizzled on the stove. Sliced, buttered bread waited on the table.

"Well kiss me blue, what is all this?" I smiled.

"I just feel better today. Jesus be praised. I realized I hadn't done anything for you in quite a while and decided to cook something up like I used to."

I walked over and hugged her from behind as she dumped the diced onions into the skillet.

"It looks wonderful, dear, thank you." I kissed her neck.

"Where have you been? I was afraid you wouldn't make it home before supper got cold."

I thought a moment. "Had to clear out the irrigation ditch, then ole Charlie stopped by to see how we were doing."

"That was sweet of him. May God bless his soul."

"Yep."

After our pleasant dinner, I hoped we could end the night in bed together. I took off my boots and socks then led her by the hand to the bedroom. We embraced and kissed, but when I touched her breast, a look of revulsion spread across her face. She pushed me away.

"Didn't you learn the last time we did this, David? Don't you remember what happened? I've gone through hellish torment because of what we've done." She stood with clenched fists, eyes wide and threatening.

"Sarah, I meant no harm. I thought it'd be nice to be together again. It's been too long for both of us." My voice was calm, but anger drained my patience, partially from her outburst and partially from my frustration.

"You have no idea what those devils want us to do. Fornicate. Live for the flesh rather than for Jesus. Lucifer wants you to plant your wicked seed in me so I give birth to another demon spawn."

"Sarah, we're married. We can have children as husband and wife. Even Reverend Talmage has four children. Children aren't wicked." I strained to keep my tone under control.

"God commanded the reverend to have those four children. I don't remember Him saying anything to you or me." She glared. "I must repent of all the misdeeds I've done."

With a sudden eruption of rage as if a mental dam had finally burst, she cried out, "You drove me to kill that child, David!" Wide-eyed horror crossed her face.

Composing herself, Sarah said with a calm voice, "No one must know what I did." She sat on the bed and hummed "Amazing Grace." My wife swayed side to side while her arms drew up into a cradling position.

The blood drained from my face. My fingertips went numb and my knees buckled. I fought to understand the meaning of her words. Buzzing filled my mind.

"You…you what?" I asked, my voice high and quivering.

"David." She smiled. "Jesus loves you. He will forgive your sins."

I felt tremors moving through my body. The cooing of a baby filled my head. I couldn't focus on her demented, grinning face without wanting to hit her until she had no face left.

*****

Deep down I always knew she hadn't told me the whole story. The umbilical cord, when I removed it, was wound so tightly around the neck it depressed the skin. Could she have done that to our sweet Mary? Or had hysteria caused Sarah to blame herself? I suppose she had gone completely mad during the pregnancy. I remembered she held blankets and pretended they were babies, her sleepless nights, and wandering phantom-like through the dark house. When sleep did come, she would jump awake muttering about nightmares. I didn't realize it wasn't a part of carrying a child.

Sarah stayed in the bedroom. I went to the kitchen and sat at the table, thinking about what she said. *You drove me to kill that child*, slammed to my mind. I shook my head, attempting to rid myself of her statement. I retrieved her Bible from the rocking chair, hoping it would bring some peace. I should have known better. Maybe Jesus could have brought some comfort, but God took him away, too. We would have his spirit with us, the Good Book said. I thought about that for a while.

After my contemplations, I stood and retrieved a lantern. I lit it, crept to the bedroom door, and peered in. An occasional twitch under the blanket indicated Sarah slept. I walked back to the kitchen and over to the cellar door. My mind retraced those first steps to Mary's temporary tomb. I remembered ants crawling on her tiny body, picking her up, carrying her to the cart. Every detail of that sickening night came with exquisite clarity.

I stood at the bottom of the stairs, jolted from my reflections. During my roaming, a piece of coiled clothes line caught under my toenail and ripped it back. I loosened the rope and rubbed my stinging toe. As I knelt in the gloom, ghostly images danced in the darkness...and then the cooing. I ascended the stairs, returned to bed and lay atop the covers.

Sarah didn't move. I held my breath. Blood throbbed in my ears. I moved closer to her. Nothing. She was warm and still. So calm, so beautiful when she slept. I stroked her face and hair.

"I love you, Sarah, my dear angel," I whispered.

I took the rope from the cellar out of my pocket. Looping it around Sarah's neck, I drew it tight. She awoke, clawing at the cord, eyes bulging. Sarah struggled and bucked underneath me.

"It's okay, my darling. This is how God works. He takes away the meek and mild so they remain immortal in spirit."

It didn't take much longer for her to settle back down to sleep.

I stayed on top of her for a few minutes, smelling her. Slowly, I unwound the twine from her neck. The creases ached where the rope had bitten into my hands. While massaging the pain, I saw my little Mary. A hazy small figure, insubstantial really, crawled toward me from the edge of the bed. I rolled over to rest parallel to my departed wife. A soft pressure moved between Sarah and me. It stopped. I closed my eyes when the weight settled close to my shoulder. Sarah was dead, yet tender baby breath fell upon my cheek.

BAD TIMES
FOR THE PECOS KID

Lee Pierce

"**S**on of a bitch," said the startled man looking down at the two tiny holes in his bright red Saturday night on-the-town shirt. He raised his head to stare at who had ruined his new shirt. The hombre stood a few feet away, a six-shooter smoking in his hand.

"Son of a bitch," he said again and fell back against the bar. His knees buckled, and he slid to the floor.

The shooter, a slender young man around five and a half feet tall, ejected two spent cartridges from his six-gun and replaced them with fresh loads. His dark eyes roamed the silent barroom, staring hard at any man who dared make eye contact.

"My name is Billy Shortridge," he announced. "I just shot and killed the famous shootist, Curley Bassham. That makes me the fastest gun in Pecos County, Texas. So, I reckon you boys can call me the Pecos Kid."

16

Billy paused a moment to let that sink in. "Is there anybody in this saloon that don't agree with what I just said?"

The place was quiet as a whorehouse on Sunday morning.

Billy strode over to the dead man's body. He reached down and fumbled through his victim's pockets. What money he found he pitched on top of the bar. Unbuckling the worn gun belt, he jerked it from the dead man's waist. A bone handled .36 Navy revolver still rested in the holster. Billy wrapped the gun belt around itself and placed it on the bar next to the money.

"Bartender," said Billy, "how much you give me for this here shootin' rig?"

The barkeep gave the rig a once-over. "I could give you, maybe, twenty dollars for it," he said. "That'd be about it."

"I'll take it." Billy turned to face the dozen or so patrons in the saloon. "That twenty, along with the twenty-seven Curley don't need anymore, will buy a right smart passel of drinks for anybody who wants to have a snort with the Pecos Kid."

A few men spoke up in the affirmative. One man who was about the kid's height but fifty pounds heavier stepped out of the crowd and ambled up to Billy.

"I'd be right proud to drink with anyone who can sling iron like you," said the fat man, smiling. "Come on boys. What do you say? Are y'all gonna join us at the bar or not?"

The crowd relaxed and began to buzz like bees in a hive about the gunfight as they bellied up to the bar. Some of them slapped Billy on the back and mumbled their congratulations.

The small bar quickly filled up with freeloaders jostling each other for a drink. Amos Quisenberry, the fat man, stayed right next to Billy. Two men dragged the body of the recently deceased into a corner to make more room at the bar. Ol' Nichols, the saloon swamper, settled in at the feet of the dead man. He commenced to pry off the corpse's boots, hoping to God they would fit him. With a little luck, the shirt and pants would too. The blood would wash out and a needle and thread would make the shirt look good as new.

Billy beamed at the adulation being heaped upon him. He'd always wanted to be a known gunfighter. Hell, fast as he was, it was his destiny.

As the whiskey and beer flowed, Amos kept it up at the kid's ear, going on about what a fine privilege it was to be in the presence of such a soon-to-be-famous man. All the while he poured down more than his share of free liquor while watching the bartender out of the corner of his eye. When it looked like the drink money was dwindling down, Amos cleared his throat.

"'Scuse me there, Jim," he said to the bartender in a loud voice. "About how much of that blood money is left? Us fellers appreciate the Pecos Kid's hospitality. We don't want to drink up any more than there is money to pay for it."

"Mr. Kid," Amos said looking as serious as he could with that ripe tomato face of his. "We all are surely obliged to you for sponsoring this here fandango, and there ain't a soul in here who wouldn't be honored to buy you a drink tonight."

Billy's face opened up in his most benevolent smile.

"Only thing is, Mr. Kid, most of us ain't worked in a mighty long spell. With the mines closed down and the ranchers around here having more hands than they know what to do with." He rubbed his belly. "Well, dang it, sir, there ain't no jobs to be had and we ain't got no money."

Billy got a puzzled look on his face but remained silent. He had no idea where this massive glob of an idiot was going with his gibberish. It was time to hit the trail, anyway. He had a reputation to uphold.

Amos ignored the kid's befuddlement and blabbered on.

"Just so's you know, we all been quite some time down on our luck and we want you to understand how much this little drink fest has meant to us."

The smile reappeared on Billy's face. What a sorry bunch of whiners he had shared his money with. He glanced towards the door when the full-winded blowhard started up again.

Amos motioned for Billy to lower his head. In a voice barely above a whisper, he spoke into Billy's right ear. "Mr. Kid, you've been so good to us I hate to have to tell you this, but you deserve to know the truth."

"What truth?"

"Now, most of these boys in here are okay fellers, but they ain't real bright. They done spent most of their time underground diggin' whatever there was to dig." Amos cleared his throat. "They work, spend their money on whiskey and whores, and work some more. It's a sad thing, but it's all they know. Myself, I've been a sight more fortunate than them. I've traveled some and seen the elephant more'n once."

Amos paused, took a deep breath and let it out in one long-drawn out sigh.

"What the devil are you gettin' at?" asked Billy.

"Well, Mr. Kid, the fact is the man you killed ain't Curley Bassham."

Billy dropped his beer mug. It hit the bar, bounced once and beer shot into the air. Ignoring the mess, he stared at Amos. "Naw, that ain't right," he said. "I seen him before. I killed Curley Bassham."

"You killed his little brother, Punt. They look nearly alike, but poor ol' dead Punt wasn't right in the head. He tried to act like his big brother, but he weren't no gunman. Hell, I never even seen him pull his iron on another man. Truth is, I don't think he could."

Billy's mind started jumping around like a spooked jackrabbit. "You're wrong," he said. "The man I killed had to be Curley Bassham, the fastest gun in this part of Texas."

"Son," said Amos, sounding real fatherly, "you killed Punt Bassham who never harmed a livin' soul. And the worst of it is you shot him down in cold blood. You murdered him."

A wild-eyed look came over Billy's face and he began to squirm like a beaver in a trap. Sweat dripped off his nose and puddled on the bar.

"There's two other things you need to know, Mr. Kid." Amos's round red face began to soften to a rosy pink. "The first thing is that

19

Punt was Curley's favorite brother. The second thing is I've seen the real Curley handle a six-shooter, and you ain't a flyspeck on a horse's ass compared to him. Yes, sir, I 'spect when he finds out what you done, he's gonna hunt you down and shoot you like a hydrophoby dog."

"I ain't afraid of him," said Billy looking none too sincere.

"Oh. I know you ain't," said Amos. "We all seen you ain't afraid of nothin'."

The fear in Billy's eyes contradicted Amos's last statement. He was scared silly. What the crowd in the saloon didn't know was that he almost didn't go through with the gunfight. Once he had called Bassham out, he wanted to turn and run out of the saloon. All those days practicing shooting at cans and tree limbs hadn't prepared him to face a man who could shoot back. If he could find a way out of this fix, he would do it in a heartbeat.

Amos must have been reading the kid's mind. "Say, there, young'un, you are sweatin' a barrelful. Are you all right?"

"Uh, yeah, I'm okay. It's a little hot in here, and, besides, I just killed a man."

"You sure done that," bellowed Amos slapping Billy on the back. "Well, Mr. Kid, we best be gettin' over to the hotel and findin' you a room."

"A room. What for?"

"Curley will be gunnin' for you, and you won't get no rest 'til you face him and shoot it out. Might as well wait for him here in town and when he shows up get it over with."

"But, I was plannin' to move on today." Billy trembled. It took what little nerve he had left to keep him from running out the door and riding away.

"Of course," said Amos scratching his face with fat stubby fingers, "there might be another way, but I doubt a man like you would want to take it. You could skedaddle out of here right now. Us fellers, bein' grateful for your generosity and all, could make up a big ol' whopper. We could tell Curley some big, ugly, scar-faced varmint shot Punt, and then forked his bronc and rode west, hell for leather."

Billy stood silent for a moment. "I don't think I can do that," he said. "I shot the man's brother and I reckon I have to take my medicine."

"Suit yourself," said Amos. "You won't have long to wait. Curley's due in town in about an hour. He's supposed to meet his brother here."

"I…In about an hour?" Billy said owl-eyed.

"Uh, huh, maybe less."

All at once, the thought of toiling away on his daddy's farm didn't sound too bad. Billy made a snap decision. "Mr. Quisenberry, I'm takin' your advice and I'm goin' back home, but you have to give me your word not to tell Curley Bassham I killed his brother."

An odd twinkle flashed across Amos's eyes, and his chubby face broke into a broad grin. "Mr. Kid, I give you my word Curley Bassham will never hear your name."

"I'm obliged to you," said Billy.

"It's the least I can do for the Pecos Kid." Amos slapped Billy on the back again.

"There ain't no more Pecos Kid," said Billy. "From now on I'm just plain Billy Shortridge, brown dirt farmer."

"Farmers don't wear no gunfightin' rigs," said Amos, winking at the bartender. "You best leave that outfit with me for safe keepin'."

"But I saved up a year to buy this six-gun and holster."

"All right," said Amos frowning, "but I can't guarantee somebody won't see you leavin' town with that rig on and squeal to Curley. He's a pretty smart feller. Might put two and two together and come up with who really shot Punt."

Billy rubbed his sweating hands together. "Okay, I reckon you're right. But how am I gonna get my money back for my rig?"

"We'll keep it here in the saloon 'til the trouble blows over. Then you can ride back and claim it."

"I don't know about that." Billy began to waver on his decision to run away before the real Curley Bassham rode into town. He wasn't sure he would ride this way again and the gun rig had set him back a pretty penny.

All of a sudden, Amos Quisenberry hollered. "Dang it! I thought I just heard somebody say they saw Curley ridin' into town from the west."

Billy jumped like he'd been blasted with double-ought buckshot. He shucked his gun belt and disappeared out the saloon doors in a dead run. In a moment, hoof beats clattered on the hardscrabble street rapidly fading into the east.

"Whooee," spouted Amos, "that boy can flat-out run when he has to. I don't recollect ever seein' nobody move that fast before."

"Somethin' else, too," said Jim the bartender, drawing a fresh beer and setting it in front of Amos. "I never saw anybody pull iron faster than that boy, either."

Amos nodded his head. "Say, Jim, how many drinks can we get for this here gunfightin' rig?" He laid the six-gun and holster on the bar.

"Now, Amos," said Jim. "I already traded for one outfit today. I ain't sure I can afford another one."

"Look at it this way, Jim. You'll own both gun rigs. Shucks, I bet you can charge folks two bits a piece to get a look at 'em."

"You think so?"

"Why sure, just think of it. You'll have two gunfighters' rigs to show; one that belonged to Curley Bassham and the other that belonged to the mysterious stranger that plugged him. Shucks, Jim, I bet it'll make this saloon famous."

Amos smiled and handed the gun belt to Jim, who placed it next to the other one.

"Okay," said Jim, "two drinks for everybody, and remember, I'll be countin'."

"I'll take a beer and a shot of whiskey," said Amos.

Leaning against the bar, he looked toward the corpse in the corner and watched ol' Nichols clomping around in new boots, the dead man's pants and shirt slung across his bony shoulders.

"Hey, there," said Amos, "a couple of you boys help get rid of that stinkin' body. I swear, as bad as Curley Bassham smelled when he was alive, he smells a heap worse when he's dead.

A DAY IN THE LIFE OF MARYANNE WINSLOW

Roberta Summers

Maryanne Winslow hitched her dapple-gray mare to a small aspen tree and waded through wild flowers so high they reached her knees. She walked with purpose toward an elderberry bush bent from the weight of its purple fruit. After checking on them every few days for the past month, she'd determined that today the berries would be fully ripened and bursting with flavor. She spread an old flannel sheet out and unsheathed a heavy knife to cut the branches before gathering as many as she could carry. She paused only to wipe the sweat from her forehead with the sleeve of her dress. It was an unusually hot day in Colorado's high country.

She tied the corners of the sheet together and hefted the bundle over her shoulder. Maryanne was by no means a tiny woman. Born of Scandinavian pioneer stock, she was tall and sturdy. When she arrived back at the ranch cabin, her nine-year-old daughter Julia would busy herself pulling berries from their stems and help her make jelly.

Maryanne left Julia behind, tending to household chores and keeping an eye on her brother, six-year-old Theron Junior.

Maryanne hung the makeshift bag to the saddle horn and mounted the mare. A low rumble of thunder echoed over the pine trees on the mountain that rose between her and home. She'd have to hurry to stay ahead of a morning rain.

"C'mon, Matilda." She flicked the reins across the horse's withers urging her to a lope. Maryanne's straw hat flew from her head, releasing a pile of lustrous auburn hair. Only calico ties kept the hat from landing in the tall grass. It bounced on her back in rhythm with the mare's pounding hoofs.

Black thunderheads roiled nearer the treetops as Maryanne reached the crest of the last rise before descending into the narrow valley. Her husband had built their ranch on a creek that emptied into Trout Lake. The forested slopes above were resplendent with rippling streams and lush grass. The cold, crystalline waters provided an abundance of fish for the small family.

Maryanne slowed her mare and cocked her head. She wondered why smoke wasn't rising from the chimney. She had told Julia to keep the fire up so the pot of soup she'd prepared that morning could simmer all day.

"Now, why doesn't that child do as she's told?" As the mare picked her way down the slope, Maryanne scanned the corrals that penned their dairy cows. Her husband, Theron wasn't in sight. Apprehension skittered up her spine. Something was not right. Caution prompted her to slow Matilda so she could approach the ranch yard quietly. Looking at the out-buildings and fields, she searched for evidence of something out of order. Her unease heightened. If Theron wasn't in the ranch yard, he should be in the fields. And where were the horses?

A gust of wind let her know the rain would start any moment. She eased her heels into the flanks of the dapple gray to press her to move a little faster. Nearing the house, Maryanne saw the door was open. She reined Matilda in, slid off the horse, and left her ground tied.

24

She tip-toed across the wide porch and peered in the door. The horror within brought her to her knees.

Theron's body dangled from a low rafter. Entrails spilled out of him to the floor and dragged in a pool of blood as he swayed in the breeze.

Maryanne wretched—vomit mixed with the offal and blood. Wild-eyed, she searched the room for her children.

Forcing herself to her feet, she went into the bedroom. Julia lay motionless with her torn dress pulled up over her head. Maryanne tugged at the blue flowered calico, revealing Julia's face. Her lifeless eyes stared at the ceiling and her blonde braids were soaked in blood. Julia's throat had been cut. Maryanne pulled the garment down to cover her daughter's violated nakedness. A spasm in her chest doubled Maryanne over in pain. Tears flowed down her cheeks.

Where was her son? He was nowhere in the house. Outside, mindless of the pelting rain, she searched for any sign of him. She walked through the side door to the barn. When her eyes adjusted to the dim light, she looked around. It appeared to be empty, but as she turned to leave, she saw her son hanging on the wall, impaled by a hay hook. Gus, the black and white dog that was always on his heels lay dead at his feet.

Maryanne lifted her son, hook and all, from the wall. Wincing, she pulled the hook from his back, carried him to the house and laid him by his sister. She pushed his unruly red curls back from his forehead. "There, my sweet baby." Painful choking sobs threatened to close her throat. She balled her fist and pressed it against her mouth. Turning her back on the grisly scene, she left the room

Maryanne dragged a chair next to her husband, stood on it and cut him down. A dull thump spread through the room as his legs crumpled underneath and the heavy weight of his body hit the floor. Mindless of her dress, she knelt in the bloody pool to stuff his entrails back into him. Her efforts were futile. Tears fell into the cavity as she swallowed waves of bile rising in her throat. In despair she sat back on her heels.

25

"I can't put you back together."

She rose and went outside to her mare. Pulling the bundle loose from the horn, she untied the knot and shook out the elderberries. Maryanne spread the sheet next to Theron and dragged him onto it. Wrapping the cloth as tightly as possible, she tied dishtowels around the sheet to secure it and keep his spilled intestines with the rest of his body.

Maryanne fetched a shovel and went to the apple tree she had planted ten years ago, right after they were married. She'd just turned eighteen and glowed with energy and happiness. Now she was digging a grave for her family. She worked in a slow rhythm driving the shovel again and again into the black loamy soil. Her face was white with shock as she went about the task of preparing the burial site. Rain mixed with her tears, which she blotted away now and then with her muddy skirt.

The sun burst through the clouds as Maryanne walked to the barn—the rain was over. She picked up the dog. Blood from the bullet wound stained the white spot on his head. She carried him out and laid him beside the grave.

Back in the house, Maryanne rummaged through a cedar chest to find a crocheted tablecloth she'd inherited from her grandmother. "This is fitting to wrap Julia in."

She pulled an afghan from the back of her rocking chair, the chair where she'd nursed both her babies. The memory brought more tears. She'd knitted the cover during her first pregnancy.

She swaddled Theron Junior in the colorful afghan and Julia in the tablecloth, then carried her children one by one to the grave.

Maryanne rolled her husband's body onto the double-wedding ring quilt that had served as their bedspread and dragged him to the open hole. There was no way she could lower such a large man gently. He fell with a thud.

Next she kissed her daughter's forehead. Holding the edges of the tablecloth shroud, she lowered Julia on top of her father. Then she knelt and placed Theron Jr. next to Julia. Last, the dog—all of her family in one grave.

Leaning back on her heels she looked at the sky and wailed a single time, "Why?" She rose and walked to the meadow and gathered all the wild flowers she could carry. She dropped four flowers onto the bodies before shoveling dirt over them. The first shovel full was the hardest. A choking pain clutched her throat and chest.

After patting down the black soil with the back of the shovel, she laid the rest of the flowers on the mound. She returned the shovel to the barn and walked to the creek where she stripped off her bloody, gore-saturated clothes and sat down in a pool. Submerged, Maryanne stayed under the water until her lungs were bursting. Thoughts of never surfacing crossed her mind, but she sat up and scratched up a handful of sand from the stream bed. She scrubbed herself, but no matter how hard she pressed the sand to her skin she couldn't feel it.

Naked, she walked to the corrals and swung wide all the gates. She opened the barn doors and herded the cattle through the corral into the ranch yard. Then she shooed all the chickens out of the coop and turned the pigs out of the sty. She seized a pitchfork, climbed the ladder to the hayloft and pitched all the hay down onto the ground. Finally, she opened the lid to the grain bin.

Maryanne led Matilda to the watering trough and let the mare loose to graze. She went into the house skirting the pool of blood and went into the bedroom where she dressed in her husband's shirt and pants and pulled on boots.

Returning to the kitchen she slid the table aside and pried up a floor board that was hidden by a braided rag rug. Groping around underneath, her fingers found an oilskin bag. She pulled it out, loosened the strings and looked in at the gold coins that had been in hiding there for the past ten years—her dowry and later on her inheritance added to it.

Laying out a dishtowel, Maryanne loaded it with biscuits and jerky from Theron's last deer kill. She ate as she worked—not because she was hungry, but knowing she'd need the energy—then tied the four corners together to make a bundle. Armed with a rifle, ammunition, the gold and food, she mounted Matilda.

Maryanne's father had taught her to track game, so if she was alert and cautious and the murderers didn't make it to town, she would find them.

First, she scouted for signs of horses leaving the ranch which she found at the beginning of the wagon track road. None of the Winslows had left the ranch for three weeks and no one had visited, so this disturbed ground would have to be from wild animals or horses. Hoping to find further tracks, she followed the double ruts. There, a lump of grass dug up, probably from a horse's hoof.

Who had done this horrific deed? Indians? We've never had trouble with Indians. Whites? Colorado had always felt like a safe, peaceable place. Regardless, whoever had slaughtered her family would pay. She would hunt them down if it took the rest of her life.

Maryanne kept Matilda to a walk as she scanned the ground. The chewed-up dirt told her the men appeared to have urged their horses to a gallop. The horses were shod, which meant white men. They had stolen two of the Winslow's horses which would most likely be on leads. That would slow their progress. She wondered if the men had picked up the pace when the rain began and if they'd counted on it to cover their tracks. She could follow their trail today—but if it rained again, maybe not tomorrow.

Matilda whinnied and shied sideways. Maryanne leaned forward to place a soothing hand on the horse's neck. "What is it, old girl?" All of Maryanne's senses were on edge. A gentle tug on the reins signaled the mare off the trail toward a stand of aspen. Deep in the grove she slid off her horse, stroking the dapple gray as she listened. She looped the reins around a tree, eased the rifle out of its scabbard, and slung the strap over her shoulder. Weaving through the trees, she neared a meadow.

The sun hung low in the sky, casting long shadows. Shivering aspen leaves formed more shadows and their constant rustle made enough background noise to disguise any misstep breaking a twig. Soon it would be dark. In the distance, water chattered over pebbles as the creek made its way downhill—more sound to cloak her footfalls.

Moving deeper into the aspens, she headed for the stream. The foliage and trees were thicker near the water and she could use them for cover.

What was that? Maryanne stopped. *Laughter?* Careful to stay near the creek, she made her way toward the voices. The golden flicker of firelight illuminating white bark on the aspens made her freeze. Holding her breath, narrowing her eyes, she stared trying to make out the shapes. She didn't want to get near the horses. They might whinny and give her away. *I need to get closer.* Slipping the rifle strap off her shoulder she cocked the gun and held it in front of her. One careful, silent step at a time, she neared the campfire.

The camp was in a little clearing where the creek made a bend. The smell of fish frying and coffee boiling blended with the aroma of wood fire smoke. The pungent odors were strong against the clean mountain air. The men made no pretense of hiding out, or of fearing reprisal.

As she moved through the shadows, she counted three of them. A tall, thin bearded man was tending to the fish. Two more were stretched out on the ground using their saddles as head rests and smoking thin cigars. Smoke curled above the head of a small wiry looking man. The other was fat and wore a greasy leather vest. *Are there others?* Beyond, she saw the horses, including her stolen ones, grazing near the stream. Fortunately, they were too far away to react to her presence.

The men were talking and laughing. Easing down onto her haunches, she turned her head sideways to catch the men's conversation.

"You shoulda seen the look on that farmer when he saw you humping his girl."

Maryanne covered her mouth with her hand to stifle a gasp.

"Wish I had, but I was a little busy. Best piece I got in a long time." This was followed by the sharp sound of a hand slapping leather chaps, accompanied by a low chuckle. "He'd a like ta kill me iffn you didn't gut him and string him up."

So it was you. Bastard.

A third voice. "Thought that dog was going to eat me alive out there in the barn," the little wiry one said. "What in the hell were you doin' with the girl while I was after them thar horses? In there havin' all the fun?"

"You know, ba dum, ba dum—gettin' a little young stuff." He made an obscene motion with his pelvis, and his laugh was a snort through his nose. "I'd a brung her along if she hadn't screamed so much."

Maryanne slumped against a tree with her knees pulled up to her chest. Tears washed her cheeks.

That animal on my beautiful girl.

She wanted to sob and howl out her pain. Instead, rage replaced her grief. She knew how to stalk animals. She took several long deep breaths, picked up her rifle and checked her knife to make sure it would slide easily out of its sheath.

If I go in shooting, I could kill one, maybe two—but not three. Outrage and horror buzzed like a swarm of hornets in her mind. She shook off the feeling. *I've got to keep a cool head. Think of them as wolves. They would take a lamb from its mother and run off.* She caught her breath. *They'd killed her little lambs.* She blinked back tears. Wolves were dangerous in a pack, but easy enough to pick off one at a time.

"Gotta take a leak." The *wolf* who said he'd raped Julia announced. He started walking toward her.

Adrenaline surged through Maryanne. She stepped behind a large tree, laid her gun on the ground with care and pulled out her knife. She heard him coming closer. He was less than three strides from her. He kept coming, then he stopped, turning his back to her, oblivious to her presence. He reeked of cigar smoke, booze and sweat, and swayed as he unbuttoned his pants. Without a second thought, Maryanne reached for his hair with her left hand and slashed his throat open. *No more trouble than bleeding a deer.* He didn't even moan. *Rape my daughter, you won't rape anyone else.*

Realizing the other two men would wonder what happened and start looking for him, she made her way back to the waiting Matilda.

30

Soon, the men would know they were hunted. They'd start looking for her or break camp and hightail it. She needed to think and be prepared for one or the other. Shaking all over, she buried her face against the mare's neck, letting the horse's clean smell replace the man's stink. Maybe she should have stayed with the body. If only one came looking, she could have killed him too. Then the sound of rifle fire wouldn't matter and she could still get the last one.

Matilda nickered which brought Maryanne into action. She shoved the rifle into its scabbard. Her judgment clouded with emotion. She hadn't planned this well. *Calm down.*

She heard a man call, "Hank, hey, Hank, what the hell you doin' out there?"

They'll find his body. She led Matilda back toward the wagon track. She wanted to be on the other side of it and ahead of them.

"Hank, the fish's done. Come 'n eat."

Crossing the road, Maryanne looked for a wildlife trail. The moon had just come up. It was only a quarter, but it gave her enough light to see. On her trips to town, she'd seen pathways through the thickets that animals had made on their way to the creek. *Ah, here's one.* She turned Matilda, and they made their way up the trail. Maryanne stopped now and then to get her bearings. Surely the men had found the body by now.

There was a rise ahead with a craggy boulder near the road. It would make a good place for an ambush. It was just across the meadow and through another aspen grove. Calculating she was out of earshot, she urged Matilda to a gallop and they were soon across the open space and back into the trees. Reining the mare to a halt, she dismounted and tied her to a branch.

With her rifle out, Maryanne started to climb. In the moonlight she could make out the two ruts that defined the wagon tracks just below. A sound caught her attention. Horses coming at a high gallop. She braced herself against the rock and shouldered her rifle. *Here they come. Just get one. Concentrate on just getting one.* One-hundred yards away. Her finger was poised. *They're coming fast.* Despite the coolness of the night, beads of sweat formed on her upper lip. She licked at a droplet. The horseman on the right was in her sights. She held her breath and squeezed the trigger. Her heart pounded in her ears. *Did I get him? Yes!*

He was being dragged along the ground by one foot caught in the saddle's stirrup. The panicked horse ran between the aspens, hurling the man against the trunks. She must have got a clean shot—he wasn't fighting to save himself. The other rider whirled his mount around. When he saw his companion, he spurred his horse and galloped off. It was almost twenty miles to the nearest town. He couldn't push his horse to go that far, especially not at night.

Maryanne half-ran and half-slid downhill and dashed along the backside of the rise to where Matilda stood munching on a tuft of grass. Out of breath, Maryanne braced her hands on her knees and sucked in a gulp of air before untying the horse's reins and swinging up into the saddle. When she emerged from the trees, she urged her mare to a trot. It was a short ride across the meadow to the road where she prodded Matilda to a gentle lope. She didn't want a full gallop. It was too dark and the horse wouldn't be able to keep up the pace.

Maryanne slowed the mare to a walk now and then to allow her to catch her breath. She needed Matilda for the long haul and didn't want to come upon her enemy unexpectedly.

Slowing with care to round a bend, she found a horse—riderless. It was one of hers, a roan gelding she'd named Red. He was holding one hoof up and his breathing was labored. Maryanne looked around. She could be a sitting duck. The horse nickered. She was off Matilda in a flash.

Yanking the gun out, she led the mare to the side of the road and into the trees. The reality of her becoming the hunted instead of the hunter sharpened her senses. She crouched down and watched Red, wondering if his leg was broken or sprained. She wanted to care for him, but it was too risky. Where did that guy go? He could be anywhere, even behind her. She whirled around. Squinting, she concentrated on looking at every shadow, rock, tree and shrub, turning full orbit. She suspected he might have gone looking for the creek which was on the other side of the road. He might want to stay near it as a source of water as he worked his way downstream toward a town. Or was he going back to get another horse? How would she manage to get near him with Matilda?

Knowing the mare would need food and water, she didn't want to leave her here. And what was she going to do about Red? Not wasting much time on thinking, she decided to lead both horses to the creek and turn them loose where they would have grass and water. It was a chance, but one she was willing to take. She hoped her gelding's leg wasn't hurt so bad he couldn't limp along on three legs. She tugged on Matilda's reins to get her to follow. As she approached, Red nickered again, but didn't move. Maryanne reached up for the reins lying on his neck. Her voice was soft. "Come along, you can do it."

Red took a tentative step, attempting to put weight on his injured leg. He whinnied in apparent pain. Maryanne ran her hand down his cannon bone. She didn't think the leg was broken. She continued a stream of low conversation, coaxing him along, aware that someone may have a gun trained on her back as she faced the horse and talked him through every step.

When the sound of the creek swelled, she unsaddled both horses, took their bridles off and stashed the tack in a thicket of bushes. "You're on your own now. There's plenty to eat and drink here. You'll be all right." She loaded her pockets with food, bullets, a few of the gold coins and hid the rest. Giving Matilda a pat, she whispered, "Look after Red, old girl," picked up her rifle, and made her way downstream slipping through the shadows. She looked up to check the position of the moon—must be near midnight.

Emotion had drained Maryanne, but anger still fueled her, and now the fear of being stalked overrode shock and grief. *Where was he?* She dodged trees, surveying her surroundings before every step. *A meadow. No protection here.* Would darkness shroud her enough for her to make it across? She hoped for a cloud to obscure the bright moon for one minute, just one minute.

Wouldn't you know. Clear sky. Not a cloud anywhere. Should I stay here? Or should I chance it?

She crouched into a low running position and dodged rocks and clumps of bushes to get to the aspen grove on the other side. A ping and shower of shattered rock. *Someone is shooting at me. From where?* She straightened to run faster. Speed, she needed speed. But was she running toward her enemy?

Gaining the grove, she threw herself onto the ground. Another bullet bit a chunk out of the tree above her head. She sat up and shouldered her rifle. He knew where she was. But, where was he?

Move farther into the trees. Maryanne wove her way through the aspens, moving away from the stream while hugging the largest trees for cover. *Let me think. Would he go to where he last aimed to see if he'd hit me?*

Can I climb any of these trees? I need a vantage point. Most of the large aspens didn't have branches low enough. And those that did were too small to climb. *There—a Ponderosa pine—perhaps?* She could barely reach the first limb of the huge tree, but there were enough broken nubs of branches close to the trunk to provide her with a foothold. She climbed to the lowest limb and pulled herself up to the next level of branches. She wasn't well-hidden, but she could see if anyone approached. Now she would wait. The night had turned cold. Her fingers were stiff. She blew on them to keep them nimble. Occasionally, she heard movement through the trees. Could be a deer or some other animal, or it could be him?

She was about ready to give up her treetop vigil when she heard a twig snap. She raised her rifle and flicked off the safety. When he came into view, she pressed her cheek against the stock of the rifle and drew a bead on him through the sight of the barrel. He was close—looking up into the tree. *Can he see me?*

He raised his pistol and aimed. She squeezed the trigger.

Simultaneous explosions echoed through the grove. Blinding pain seared Maryanne's side. The impact knocked her out of the tree. She hit the ground on her back, her rifle firing on contact. He was on her in a flash. She whisked out her knife and jammed it into his side just as his fist smashed into her face. She lost consciousness.

*****

Something velvety nuzzled Maryanne's face. Light pierced her eyes as she forced them open. Matilda's nostrils came into view.

"Hello, girl," she mouthed through puffy lips.

She turned her head. She couldn't move her arm. Lying on it was a big man, and dead weight—really dead weight. Propping herself up on her free elbow, she saw that one of her bullets had torn a hole in his chest and her bowie knife was still stuck in his side. She pushed him off, pulled out the knife and wiped it on his jacket.

The murder of her family had been avenged.

She'd survived.

But what for?

ELLIE'S PLIGHT

Gloria O'Shields

"Chicken shit," eleven-year-old Ellie Fisher mumbled sitting on the back step of the ranch house. "I hate chicken shit, and I hate tromping through chicken shit." Resting her chin on a fist, with narrowed eyes she glared across the yard at the enclosure where roosters and hens were scratching up dirt and poop.

Jackson, her younger brother, poked his head out the kitchen door. "You'd better get busy collecting those eggs." Taunting, he added, "You're already in *big* trouble."

Ellie turned and gave him a dirty look. On any other morning she would have pulled him out the door and twisted his arm. But today Ellie had bigger concerns. She stood and picked up the egg basket. With her bum still numb from sitting on the ice-cold step, she adjusted the back of her jeans and set off in an awkward stride.

"You're walking funny," Jackson laughed and pointed at her. "Like you're gonna pee your pants." He smirked.

"Shut your pie hole, you little brat." Ellie continued toward the chicken coop and grunted, "If that rotten old rooster comes near me, I'm gonna kick him silly. *"*

*****

Ten minutes later Ellie shuffled into the kitchen. She set the basket of eggs on the counter and threw her winter jacket over the back of a chair next to the table.

Mrs. Fisher glanced up from crimping the crust on her prize-winning apple pie. "Check those eggs to see if any need cleaning before you put them in the refrigerator. Don't forget to leave a dozen out for me to devil later."

Jackson ran into the kitchen and stopped next to Ellie. With a hand cupped beside his mouth, he whispered in her ear, "You're going to *get it* and soon." He skipped into the living room.

Ellie studied her mother's eyes. *She doesn't look angry. When she's angry, her eyes squint.*

Mrs. Fisher finished the pie crust. She stared out the window at the snowcapped San Juan Mountains and darkening sky. "It looks like we'll have snow before nightfall." After washing her hands she turned to Ellie. "I have to go to town and pick up a few things for tomorrow, so I'd better get going before the weather turns." Mrs. Fisher wrapped the pie with tinfoil and placed it in the freezer compartment of the refrigerator. "I should be back from Durango in about two hours. You keep an eye on your brother so he stays out of trouble and don't let him peek at the gifts under the Christmas tree. Your dad is out in the barn if you need him." Within minutes Ellie's mother was on her way.

Ellie finished checking the eggs and left twelve in a bowl on the counter before leaving the kitchen.

Jackson turned his eyes away from his video game as Ellie entered the living room. "Where's Mom going?"

"To the store and I'm in charge." Ellie crossed her arms. "So watch out."

"She's probably getting paper plates." He snickered and returned to his game.

Ellie plopped down in the blue overstuffed chair near the Christmas tree knowing full well Jackson would snoop if she took her eyes off him. She tried to remain vigilant while her mother was gone. Yet, over and over her mind kept wandering to the events of earlier that morning.

*****

"Get up Ellie, it's seven o'clock," her mother called. "We've got a lot of work to do today and I need your help in the kitchen."

"Okay." She bounded out of bed, jumped into her clothes, brushed her teeth and ran downstairs.

"Breakfast is on the table," Mrs. Fisher said. "Don't gobble it down too fast. After you're done, we need to wash up the dinner dishes from last night."

Ellie remembered the night before when members of the Fisher family who lived nearby, twelve in all, had gathered for their traditional pre-Christmas dinner and game night. It had been a great evening with kids yelling, parents yelling at the kids to pipe down, and Grandma Fisher yelling at the parents to let the kids have fun.

Her mother sighed at the counter cluttered with unwashed dishes. "I'll wash, you dry. Set the dishes on the table and I'll put them away when we're done." She filled the sink with water and added a dollop of dish detergent. "Sure wish I was getting a dishwasher for Christmas."

Ellie knew her father had one stashed in the barn but resisted the urge to spill the beans.

Before long the top of the small drop leaf table was covered. Ellie pulled up a leaf and locked it in place. Soon it too was heavy with stacks of dishes. "How many more are left?" she asked turning to her mother.

"Just a couple of pots and pa…"

Boom…Crash. The kitchen table tipped over sending glasses and dishes splintering on the floor.

Mrs. Fisher spun toward the noise and threw her hands in the air "Oh, my goodness."

Ellie shook with uncontrollable sobs. "It's my fault. All our dishes are broken and it's my fault. I...I shouldn't have put so many on the leaf."

Mrs. Fisher laughed and hugged her daughter.

Tears streamed down Ellie's face. *Why is Mom laughing?* She trembled in panic. *Why is Mom laughing?*

"Don't worry sweetie, everything will be okay."

"Honest, Mom." Ellie sniffled. "I didn't do it on purpose."

"I know sweetie." Mrs. Fisher smiled. "They were old and mismatched. Don't worry. Now, come and help me clean up this mess."

After the kitchen was tidied, Ellie was sent to gather eggs while her mother peeled and sliced apples for the pie she was making.

Stalling before doing her chore, Ellie sat outside on the cold kitchen steps cursing the chickens while contemplating her plight. *What will happen when Dad finds out I broke the dishes?*

*****

Two hours later, Jackson turned off his game and set it on the end table. "You're not going to get any presents. Mom will take all your presents back so she can buy dishes for Christmas dinner. I bet that's what she is doing right now. I saw her moving the stuff under the tree while you were collecting eggs."

Heat rose to Ellie's cheeks, tears welled in her eyes. *Don't cry in front of the brat. Don't cry in the front of the brat.*

The sound of a car on the road leading to the ranch house caused Jackson to leap to his feet and look out the front window. "Mom's back. Now, you'll see, I'm right. You're getting nothing for Christmas."

A few minutes later, their mom and dad entered the living room. Ellie could no longer hold back tears when she saw her parents. A mischievous smile spread across Jackson's face.

"What's the matter?" her mom asked. "Don't cry, Ellie."

"I...I'm so sorry 'bout the dishes. I...I can earn extra money doing chores at Grandpa's to buy new ones."

Mr. Fisher put his arm around his wife's shoulder and eyed the children. "Enough," he said in a stern voice.

The children stood at attention.

"I think it is time…" he paused and grinned. "To follow our Christmas Eve tradition and everyone open one gift. Kids always go first, so pick out a present. Make sure it's your biggest one."

Jackson scrambled to the tree and picked out a large box wrapped in reindeer paper. Ellie slumped in the overstuffed chair unable to bring herself to look for a gift.

"I want to go first," Jackson stared at Ellie. "I should get to go first because I haven't done anything *bad* today."

Mrs. Fisher looked up at her husband, smiled and said, "Okay, I think he deserves to go first."

"Yes," their dad said. "After his behavior today, he should go first."

Jackson beamed as he ripped off the paper, tossing it on the floor. He pried open the box and peered inside. His expression turned sour. "Dishes!"

"Yep," Mr. Fisher said. "They've been there since last week. All the reindeer boxes contain brand new dishes and glasses for our family. Go pick one out, Ellie."

Everyone laughed as Ellie raced to the tree—even Jackson.

THE LAST RIDE

Traci HalesVass

T he sun rises, spreading light across the valley, burning off the clouds. First illuminated is the top of the mountain; the gold of fall aspens spark like fire. Then the pastures warm slowly. The sun brings out the white stallion from the shadows. He tastes the crisp piney air, nose high, then runs, mane and tail streaming behind him, breath like new formed clouds.

With his grand entrance, the mares and colts in the barn start their banging and rattling. Time to finish the coffee and feed.

The rickety steps down from the cabin's deck make Trina's hips ache. By the time she reaches the barn, her back burns and her breath is difficult to draw in. Rufus, the old red hound, and three of the cats sidle out of the barn when she pushes open the big doors. Randall must be near if Rufus is greeting her this morning. She is glad to spend a minute scratching the dog's scruffy ears and tail. He looks at her with a tilt of his head as if asking a question she won't answer.

"Mz T!" shouts Randall, tipping his beat-up cowboy hat as he walks into the barn. "After I feed, do you want to ride? Doc would like to stretch a bit."

Randall cares for the ranch and horses, earning his rent and a small salary. Trina let him drag that flimsy single-wide to the north pasture when she admitted to herself the chores were getting to be too much for her. Over the years the trailer settled into the land. At some point no one could remember, a little red puppy took up his home with Randall. Now the trees he planted tower over the top of his roof, some naked with the oncoming winter, some in glorious reds and yellows.

"Yes, Randall, I'll ride Doc, but take a break and ride with me for a little while."

"Soon's I git the feedin' done, be my pleasure to company you."

While Randall feeds, Trina makes her rounds, touching and speaking to the horses. She walks up to each warm nose, petting the velvetiness, breathing into the nostrils. Some horses she puts her cheek against, inhaling the pungent smell, rubbing her hand against warm withers, scratching a soft ear, stroking a chiseled cheek. As she turns from the last stall, she sees Randall resting on a bale, watching her. Doc and St. Marie are saddled and shifting. "Oh, sorry, didn't know I took so long."

"No prob, Mz T. You all right this morning?"

"Yes, yes, I'm fine. Just feeling a bit wistful. Ready to go? Rufus, you comin'?" But the dog starts turning circles in the loose hay, preparing for a nap. He shows his age, too.

Randall helps her mount Doc, then straddles St. Marie. They ride slowly out of the stables, cross the road, and head up the trail. For many minutes, because the path is steep and narrow, Trina rides ahead with Randall following. When they reach a flatter area where the creek pools, they loosen the reins and let the horses sip water.

"So Randall, everything running smoothly? Anything I need to take care of before I...to take care of?"

"Running fine, ma'am. Winter hay is ordered—delivered end a month. Jake scheduled to start hoof checks next week. Shots are current.

All looks good, just like we talked last week. 'Scuse me for saying, but you sure seem more worried 'bout things than usual."

Doc snickers just then and St. Marie flinches and tenses. Randall and Trina's attention snaps to the right just in time to see a fat, ringtail disappear under a red scrub oak. Trina tightens the reins and turns Doc's head. "He just doesn't like those coons, now, does he?" she says.

Randall laughs and turns his mount's head. He leads this time and Trina follows. They climb the rocky trail up the mountain. The greenwood smell of aspen fills the air, mixed with the musky scent of fallen leaves. As the elevation increases, more leaves cover the ground, and the ones still hanging onto the aspens are fading and dry. At the fork in the trail, Randall stop and waits until Trina rides up next to him.

"I would like to go to the top today, Randall, how about you?"

"Yes, ma'am. Horses seem like they could do a whole lot more."

The trail opens up wider as it leads through a meadow of variegated browns and muted colors. Tree line. A cold breeze sweeps across the meadow and both horses perk up their ears and sniff.

"I'm giving Doc his head, Randall!" Trina thumps the big horse in the flanks with both heels, her elbows in, head down. Doc picks up his pace to a trot, then breaks into a full canter.

Randall gives rein to St. Marie and soon the two horses run side by side, heads up, manes flowing, tails out straight behind them. Trina's white hair streams behind her, glistening in the autumn sun.

They slow, Trina is out of breath and Doc has worked up a lather. She gulps in air while trying to untangle her hair and work it back into its bun. When she can breathe, she laughs, "Thank you, Doc. Thank you, Randall."

"Yes, ma'am. Forgive me for sometimes forgettin' what a star rider you were…are."

"Some things you never get too old for. Let's head home."

*****

After the ride, Trina showers. She starts cleaning then; beginning in the bedroom, boxes and a trash can on the floor, fresh rags and a spray bottle of vinegar and water, furniture oil. Atop the heavy mahogany dresser sit the trophies. She picks up the smallest: "Katrina Sarts, Rodeo Queen 1964," dusts it and puts it in a box. The next: "Barrel Champion 1965." Four small trophies in all, dusted and packed. She closes cardboard flaps, tapes up the top, and labels it "Little Britches Rodeo Club."

The three larger trophies are heavier and she has difficulty wrestling them down from the dresser. A gilded horse sits atop the award, tail out, high stepping: "Dressage Champion 1970," another for '72. She hefts the largest, holding it in front of her and reading, "Lifetime Achievement Award, United States Equestrian Federation, 1978," and packs it alongside the others.

With the trophies packed, it is time to tackle the drawers. This one is nearly empty. Randall now wears most of the clothes that had been in here. Trina laughs at the memory of that day, when she realized, as Randall picked through those jeans, shirts, and sweaters, how she missed having a man around the house.

The few remaining items, a couple big sweaters, an unopened box of white handkerchiefs, and a wad of colorful ties, land in the charity box, and Trina moves on to the next dresser.

She sorts her clothing into charity and trash. There aren't many clothes. In the last few years she has whittled those down to a few pieces of comfortable wear. She hasn't gone anywhere in so long, she doesn't know why she needed more. After her last relative died, she doesn't go to anyone's funeral. Too much trouble.

In the closet, Trina leaves only her leathers, a lacy white blouse, and her favorite boots.

The living room of the cabin facing the valley is small and all windows. This time of the afternoon the sun comes in hard. If it were summer, Trina would have closed all the shades. Now, in the fall, the sun slants lower and its heat is welcome. It shines and sparks off the row of framed photos.

She glances over the faces and goes back to the kitchen to make a cup of tea. She puts off the next task—dealing with the photos.

Trina asks herself again, as she has done many times during these months of planning, why she had to clean up so much. And the answer she gives herself is because that's her way, never leaving a mess.

Her cleanliness and orderliness are traits Jordan appreciated and relied on in the business. She smiles thinking about the disorderly piles of papers she found the first time she went to his cabin.

She had taken her prize money and chosen the horse of her dreams. The best lineage for dressage with a bit of extra ruggedness for trail riding. Trina had traced both sire and dam lines, following pairings and offspring for five generations. Her search ended at a small cabin northeast of Durango, nestled in the hills between Pagosa and Del Norte.

A young man, short and bow-legged, came out of the barn to greet her, taking off his straw hat to reveal scraggly blond hat-head.

Jordan ran the family breeding company after his parents retired to Florida. When Trina told him about the foal she wanted, he was first perplexed, then intrigued. "An interesting mix," he said. "I thought this line wouldn't go nowheres."

The little filly was fuzzy and short. Trina thought maybe she'd made a mistake when she first saw her nuzzling cowardly against her mamma. Jordan whistled. The filly perked her ears, put her head up, and high-stepped over to them. The natural, smooth movement made both young people laugh.

Finding the paperwork for the pedigree was not so easy. Trina sipped Jordan's terrible coffee while he rummaged through stacks of paper. Then he made spaghetti while she sorted and organized.

She didn't remember ever leaving his place; for the next thirty years the couple worked together, breeding fine horses that Trina would ride and take prize after prize.

Not much of those times were captured in the photos. She dusts and boxes them, not knowing what to do with the pictures, not having the heart to throw any away. There was no one who would want them. The couple never had time to raise children; their family had been the horses.

Trina is tired. She decides to leave the rest—the dishes and cutlery. Those common household items Randall would use.

After a dinner she can't finish, Trina puts on the tea kettle. She changes her clothes while the water boils. The outfit still fits, though a little baggy in spots and tight in others. She puts on blush and a touch of lipstick, finishing just as the kettle whistles.

Earl Grey with a big tablespoon of honey and a drop of cream, stirred. She reaches up into the cupboard for an unmarked pill bottle. Opening two, four, eight capsules, she pours the white content into the tea.

She stirs until the powder dissolves, and sits in the big chair. The tea is bitter and Trina has a hard time swallowing, but chokes the beverage down. The hills across the pasture glow a warm brown as the sun sets.

A few golden aspens flare, then fade. Dark descends; Trina feels nothingness overtake her.

A clatter of hooves on wood and the snorting of a horse sound. Trina rises to see what is going on. The big white stallion on the porch snorts and paws restlessly, lifting one foot, then another. "Hush, Michael, hold still," the rider whispers. He holds out a gloved hand, "Trina."

"Jordan," Trina says, grabbing his hand. She slips her foot into the stirrup Jordan clears, and hops. Jordan grabs her waist, pulls her up, and places her in front of him in the saddle.

KEEPS THE BEAR WOMAN

Linda Fredericks

We rode in silence, Curtis Ten Bear and I, along the bumpy switchbacks of Wolf Mountain. Curtis picked me up earlier at the Billings bus station. It was the coldest winter in recent years; forty below with the wind chill and mounds of plowed snow everywhere. I suggested we find a liquor store to get a bottle of Baileys and a McDonald's to buy coffee before we started up the mountain. I sat on the passenger side of the pickup despite his several urgings to slide over next to him. I felt uncomfortable even though we were in Billings and I was fairly certain I wouldn't see any of my relatives. I longed for the moonlight and the stars. I knew the night sky would ease the tightness in my back and neck.

"You seem uptight," he said. "Relax, no one is going to see you if that's what you're worried about."

I wasn't worried. I just didn't want anyone knowing my business.

We were driving past Yellowtail Dam. The sun was beginning to descend below the peaks, bathing the sandstone bluffs along the dam in a cool pink that soothed my eyes. Layers of rock stacked one on top of the other like layers of time, each a different color: purple, green and pale yellow in the sandstone above the waterline.

"Those are the Big Horns way over there," he said pointing with his chin to the southeast. "And there straight ahead, see those peaks? Those are the Absarokas. Now, look along those outcroppings." His hand still around the steering wheel, he pointed with his index finger. "Right there, that's Wolf Mountain. They call this range the Pryor Mountains. They're sacred to us Crow's. You ever been up here before?"

"No, but it seems familiar." I thought the road, the way it curved, and the short clumps of cedar growing in grotesque shapes out of these eerie rock formations did look familiar but I knew I hadn't been here before."*Hetseohe mato neaseho' enehe.*"

Curtis looked at me with a serious expression and said, "English only." We laughed.

"Sorry, it means like *déjà vu*. It feels like I've been here before. I wish you could talk Cheyenne."

He said, "Yeah, well I wish you could talk Crow."

"Yeah, well that ain't gonna happen anytime soon." We looked at each other and laughed again.

I punched him on the arm, moved over next to him and put my hand on his chest. He kissed the top of my head and said some words in Crow which I knew meant "I love you."

Curtis and I met like this before; whenever I could get away from home without arousing too much suspicion. This time, I was checking out the possibility of going back to college at Eastern. I used enrolling in classes as an excuse to go to Billings. My Mom would give me some money, tell me how I should get an education, then come home and help my people. She said it was something *they* could never take away from me. I knew *they* couldn't take anything away from me anyway, with or without an education.

"Why can't you find a local boy, a nice boy from a good family, someone like Walter Limpy?" she'd say.

And I'd say, "Why can't you mind your own business?"

Then she'd get angry and say, "Don't go getting mixed up with any Crows either, you know what your dad would say about that."

So I didn't tell her about Curtis even though I wanted to.

When the Greyhound bus I took from Ashland pulled into the bus terminal, I saw Curtis right away. He was standing with his back against the white cinderblock wall inside the waiting area. Just looking at him made my back arch slightly. I was remembering when we first met over in Lame Deer, at the Veteran's Day Powwow.

I noticed him right off: his six-foot five-inch frame and his weight a perfect displacement of space. I sat on the bleachers behind his drum group and watched him sing all weekend. Then, on Sunday, when I thought he would leave Lame Deer and I'd never see him again, I used it…my bear fetish. I took it from my pocket, held it tight in my fist, felt the heart line and, before I even put it back in my pocket, he walked over to the bleachers where I was and sat next to me at the end of the bench. He made small talk about what a good powwow it had been and did I ever go to any at Crow Agency. Finally, he introduced himself. He said he had noticed me and I looked familiar. He thought maybe we had met before. I remember shaking his hand and saying my name.

"Layla Little Bear," he repeated. "I would have remembered that name."

That was a year ago last month. Since then my dreams are always the same: the bear comes to me and tells me this story.

*****

Looking at Curtis through the bus window makes me smile. His upper arms too big for the short-sleeved shirt he is wearing. It's baby blue with mother of pearl snaps down the front and on each pocket flap. A faded orange bandana is tied around his neck. His hair longer than I remember but still as black and worn in the same way, pulled back in a ponytail. He smiles too as he pushes his back off the wall and steps toward me.

"Layla," he says. He puts his arm around my shoulder and kisses the top of my head. I close my eyes. He puts on his black down jacket and zips it up.

"We're going to my little brother's cabin," he says as he bends over to get my bag. "It's only a couple hour's drive. Sound good?"

"Does it have heat?" I laugh.

"Yeah, there's a fireplace. Don't worry, I'll keep you warm." He smiles and touches my neck.

The first sip of Bailey's and coffee warms my belly.

"This is good stuff," he says. "Are you trying to get me drunk so you can have your way with me?"

"Like I need to get you drunk to have my way with you?" I look down and away from him surprised by my remark. I feel flushed and still uncomfortable.

"We've been singing a lot lately. Did you get the tape I sent you?"

"Yeah, remember I wrote you and told you I listen to it every day. I think you guys are singing really well. I've even learned a few of the songs already. My mom was asking about it. She wanted to know who sent it."

"Well, did you tell her?"

"No. You know how she feels about Crows and anyway what would I tell her? I don't know much about you yet."

*****

That wasn't altogether true. I did know a little about Curtis Ten Bear. I knew he was a Crow Indian from Lodge Grass. A Mountain Crow, from the Bear Clan, to be exact. I also knew he played football at Eastern, back when they had a football program there and I knew he did three tours in Vietnam. I also knew a few incidentals that I picked up here and there but mostly gossip. The most important thing I knew about Curtis Ten Bear was, he was a singer of the old songs. An "ole time Indian boy," as my grandma used to say, describing Indian men who, although they lived nowadays, kept their spirit in the past.

Twilight came, and the moon was now a giant golden amulet placed on the horizon like an offering. I had known of its power, especially for women, all my life. I began to relax. There was only enough light to distinguish the outlines of the trees as we continued our climb up the rim rock to Wolf Mountain. The road curved west and became steep. The pickup spun its wheels and spit rocks against the under carriage. It jerked several times then lunged forward moving like a tank up the incline.

"We're close now. It's just beyond the rim."

I saw the outline of the cabin as we reached the summit. It was nestled in a narrow clearing between two stands of Lodgepole pines. There was a corral on the south side in which I could make out the shapes of two horses. The cabin was small and looked dark and cold as we pulled up and parked in front. Curtis turned off the ignition and leaned forward to find the moon through the windshield.

"I love this place," he said. "I could live up here all the time."

"Why don't you?" I asked.

"I don't know why. I guess I'm too caught up in the town scene right now." He smiled at me. "If you want to know the truth, I'm looking for a woman who will live here with me."

"Hey, don't look at me. I'm into the town scene, too." We both laughed. "You know Curtis, sometimes I think I would like to live in a place like this but it scares me. I think the isolation would make me lonely."

The scent of pine and cedar filled my nostrils as I opened the pickup door. I sat for a moment, looking down on the miles we covered and shivered. The faint light made the distance look greater. I closed my eyes and tilted my head back to breathe in the cold air. When I opened them, I saw millions of stars and the blue-green of the northern lights. *Wihio,* the North Star, was directly overhead, pointing north to my home.

"Layla, will you get the blankets from behind the seat?"

I moved the seat forward and pulled out the blankets. I wrapped one around my shoulders and carried the others across my arms.

51

Through the rear window of the pickup I saw Curtis lift a cardboard box from the truck bed and carry it to the cabin. I moved slowly making full circles as I went. I wanted to take it all in. When I got to the cabin door, I paused to steady myself. Curtis lit an oil lamp and was kneeling in front of the huge fireplace, wadding up newspapers. It was the most beautiful fireplace I had ever seen. Made from perfectly round, precisely placed, smooth gray, river rocks. The dim light barely illuminated the interior. The front door opened to the east with two large windows on either side. There was a table and two chairs, an old-fashioned sideboard in the corner and a low bench next to the fireplace. On the hearth sat an enamel coffee pot and two cast iron frying pans nesting one inside the other.

"There's some food in the box on the table, if you're hungry."

"No, I'm fine," I said. "I'll eat something later."

Still kneeling, Curtis sat back on his heels in front of the fireplace and tapped the logs with a wrought-iron poker. I put the blankets on the table and watched him. Pulling the blanket tighter around my shoulders, I sat on one of the chairs. The fire became a blaze that howled and swirled into a funnel of burnt paper and crackling sparks. Dark elongated shadows flickered on the walls and across the ceiling.

"Have you brought any women here before?" I looked away as I said this.

He looked into the fire as he answered. "Of course not. Everything I've done since I met you, are things I've never done before." He turned toward me and smiled, then whispered, "Come here."

I moved over to the fire and knelt in front of him. He raised himself off his heels, so we were face to face. I untied the bandana from around his neck and kissed him softly.

"I've missed you, Layla Little Bear. I think about you…" His words were muffled and distant.

I thought of the legend of "Keeps the Bear Woman," *A Cheyenne woman, Wihio went among the Crows seducing the most beautiful and powerful of all their warriors, a dog soldier from the Bear Clan. She lured him away from his people to the mountains where she kept him under her spell. She then went among his clan and seduced his younger brother coaxing him to the river. With the two most powerful warriors subdued, the tribe was lost. Several from their clan traveled along the river to look for the young brother, while others searched the mountains for the older warrior. They became known as the River Crows and the Mountain Crows. They argued and fought amongst themselves and never reunited. The Crow Tribe split, humiliated by a Cheyenne woman.*

"Do you know the legend?" I asked.

"What legend?" He smiled and pulled me closer.

"The legend of 'Keeps the Bear Woman'?"

"Yeah, I've heard of it but it's not a Crow story so I don't believe it. Where are the blankets?"

"Over there on the table." I pursed my lips pointing with my chin.

He pulled the tape player from the cardboard box and gathered the blankets in his arms. He moved around the room gracefully and deliberately. I wanted to ask him what he believed in, if not the old stories, but he was a Crow and I'd never understand his beliefs.

"Here," he said as he handed me the tape player. "Rewind this. There's a song on the tape I want you to hear."

I took the tape player and sat cross-legged with it on my lap.

He knelt beside me and spread the blankets out on the floor. When the tape player finished rewinding, I pushed the play button. I didn't recognize the song. He lay on the blankets and clasped his hands behind his head. Lying beside him I rested my head in the groove below his shoulder. As I listened to the tape and watched the shadows dance on the north wall, he began to undress me slowly like the times before. The war dance songs vibrated in my ears. I pulled apart the mother of pearl snaps to see his brown chest glisten above me in the firelight. At that moment, I knew who he was and then his weight was on me.

*****

53

When I wake he's gone. Only the blankets and the cardboard box remain. I wad up newspapers to rekindle the fire. I take the jug of water from the cardboard box and pour some into the coffee pot. I set the pot on the fire and wait. When the water boils, I throw in a handful of coffee. The aroma pleases me. I feel content. I prop two blankets up against the right side of the fireplace and rest my back against them. I sit for a long time and gaze through the windows, sipping the coffee and eating some graham crackers I found in the box. The sun is low and red in the eastern sky. I find my jeans in the jumbled blankets and carefully pull the fetish from my pocket. I hold it tight in my fist. It's carved from red pipestone and the heart line is inlaid with turquoise. As I trace the line with my finger, I think about my old auntie and what she said when she passed it on to me.

"It has great power, bear medicine. I give it to you because you are a bear dreamer like me." She tells me that I must, in turn, pass it on when I am too old to make the medicine work. She said I will know who to give it to. "The bear will lead her to you as you were led to me. Keep it with you always. It will protect you on your path." She names me "Keeps the Bear Woman." I squeeze it tight again, then put it back in my pocket and pull on my jeans.

Outside the air is still and warmer than I expect. Snow crunches under my feet as I walk out into the clearing. I follow a narrow footpath along the rim rock above the switchback. There's no sign of the pickup now. The tracks covered over by the ground blizzards of the previous night. I jump down to a rock outcropping. Far below I see the Tongue River flowing north along the snow outlined contours. I reach inside my pocket and pull out the fetish one last time. I close my eyes to feel its smoothness. With the heel of my boot I chip out a small hole in the sandstone rock under my feet, just as I've done in countless dreams. I kneel down, straddling the hole with my knees, and place the fetish inside. I cover it up with loose rock and dirt, using my hands to smooth over the hole.

I remember the horses in the lodgepole corral beside the cabin and I run all the way back. I know there is someone inside when I turn the doorknob but it is too late to stop. The door is already open. For a second I think it is Curtis but I know better.

"*Sododgie*," he says. "I hope I didn't frighten you."

"No, you didn't frighten me. You must be Curt's younger brother."

"Yeah, that's right. I'm Shawn."

"It's good to meet you Shawn. I'm Keeps the Bear Woman."

"You're who?" he asks.

"Layla Little Bear."

As we shake hands I ask him about the horses. He smiles. I push my hands deep into my pockets and remember the fetish is gone, but I smile at him anyway. I see he recognizes me. I know he will go with me, and so we saddle up the horses and ride in silence, Shawn Ten Bear and I, down the cut bank to the river.

CLAUDE STOCKARD'S DILEMMA

Lee Pierce

Chapter 1

L onnie Youngblood was a hired killer. Big, ugly and mean, for the right amount of money, he would take anyone's life. The grapevine allowed as how, over the last ten years, he had done in over 30 men. Texas was his stomping grounds. His name brought fear into the hearts of the people who lived there. Late one night in 1875 he rode west out of Texas.

Dawn on his third day out found him riding into the small New Mexico village of Puerta de Luna. He stopped at the edge of town eyeing the buildings before him. Most were adobe with some wooden structures scattered about. The dusty street was empty except for a few loose dogs roaming around. He nudged the buckskin gelding he was riding. The big horse started up the street at a slow walk. Halfway through town Lonnie noticed a small bank, the Guadalupe County Bank.

"Town is big enough to have a bank," he said. "It ought to have a decent hotel and a couple of saloons." He patted his horse on the neck. "Maybe we'll stop here for a while and get some rest. What do you think, Buck?" The horse made no sound. "I'll take that as a yes, ol' pardner."

Lonnie rode until he read a sign that said Marshal's office. He guided Buck to the hitching rail out front, dismounted, and tied the big horse to the rail. Stepping up on the plank sidewalk he peered through the door before he went inside. A young man sat at a desk against a back wall. "Must be a deputy," Lonnie mumbled as he stepped inside.

The marshal's office was tiny. The place gave Lonnie a claustrophobic feeling. A half-full gun rack hung on the wall behind the desk. A Franklin stove stood in the corner. The man behind the desk looked up.

"I'm looking for the marshal."

The young man stood up. He was tall, reed thin and clean shaven. "I'm Marshal Jim Stevens. What can I do for you?

"My name is Lonnie Youngblood. Ever heard of me?"

Marshal Stevens rubbed his chin. "No, don't reckon I have. Should I know your name?"

"It's not important. I just rode in and I'm lookin' to spend some time here resting and relaxing. This a peaceable town?"

"It sure is. Why since I got elected marshal six months ago, the only people I've had to lock up are a few drunks. Puerta de Luna is a fine place to live. My wife and I are happy here."

Lonnie hitched up his gun belt. "Good. Which way is the livery stable?"

"Just down the street on the left. You can't miss it. I hope you enjoy your stay, Mr. Youngblood. If there is anything I can do, just ask." The marshal stuck out his hand. Lonnie shook it and walked out of the office.

He rode to the livery. Dismounting, he pitched a dollar to the attendant, Muley Grimes. "Rub him down and grain him," he said. "I may be here a few days. His name is Buck. Treat him right."

"Yes, sir, I will surely do that," said Muley. "He's a fine lookin' animal."

Lonnie ignored him and strode outside. He headed in the direction of a saloon he had noticed two blocks down. Being a man of the plains, he did not take well to walking. He sort of hobbled around like a man walking on rocks. Soon he reached the saloon, glad his journey ended.

The saloon was small. Six tables lay strewn about and the bar in front of the back wall was, maybe, twelve feet long. Three men sat at a corner table playing cards. Two men lounged at the bar. Lonnie sidled up to the bar and propped his foot on the rail.

"What'll she be?" said the short dumpy bartender.

"Is your beer cold?" asked Lonnie.

"No, sir, but it's a mite cool."

"Draw me a tall one. You got anything to eat?"

"I can make you a cold beef sandwich."

Lonnie grabbed the mug of beer and turned to face the card players. "Wash your hands," he said, "and make me a thick sandwich."

Behind him the bartender made a strange face and started to protest, but he ambled to the washbasin and scrubbed his hands.

Lonnie perused the room. The place was no different from a hundred other saloons he had been in, except maybe smaller. In the middle of the day smoke wasn't a problem. Lonnie knew that when the crowd showed up for the night, the smoke would be stifling. He detested smoking and was reticent to contend with it.

The men glanced up noting the big stranger's arrival. His clothes were rumpled and caked with dust, but a close observation would've found the butt of the six-gun, resting high on his right hip, clean.

A great commotion flared up out in the street followed by sporadic gunfire. A wild-eyed man half-stumbled into the saloon and hollered, "The bank's being robbed."

Everyone, including Lonnie, made a beeline for the door. Outside all hell was breaking loose. Men ran in the street, dogs barked and gunfire rang through the air. All looked east towards the bank.

Lonnie rubbernecked with the rest of them. He chuckled and said to himself, "Glad I ain't got no money in there." A streak of fire sliced the right side of his head. A scream stuck in his throat as blackness overwhelmed him and he tumbled to the ground.

Chapter 2

Marshal Stevens sprang to his feet at the sound of gunfire. He charged outside trying to figure out where the noise was coming from. Realizing the commotion came from outside the bank, he took off in that direction. "Oh, my Lord!" he said. "They're robbing the bank. This can't happen in Puerta de Luna." He drew his six-gun as he raced toward the bank.

Dust billowed in the air, obstructing the marshal's vision. He could barely make out horsemen riding west out of town. How many was anybody's guess. Shielding his eyes from the dust the marshal slowed down. He reached the bank to find a bunch of men milling around in front of it. "Out of my way!" he said. "Let me through. I'm Marshal Stevens." Pushing and pulling his way through the throng, the marshal at last made it to the banks door. Stepping inside, he holstered his pistol.

"Over here Marshal," called the bank's teller, Chesley Trotter. "Mr. Ozgood has been shot." The man's voice quivered. "I fear he is dying."

"Tell one of the men outside to go get Dr. Mullins," said the marshal. On the floor in the back of the bank next to the open vault lay the owner of the bank, Wilton Ozgood. Crimson seeped through a hole in the middle of his white shirt. Marshal Stevens knelt beside the injured man and examined the wound. It didn't look good; Ozgood had lost a lot of blood. The banker began to mutter. Marshal Stevens lowered his ear to the man's mouth.

"I recognized the leader," he whispered. "It was John Stockard." Wilton Ozgood wheezed. Blood bubbled from his lips, he shuddered and died.

Marshal Stevens closed the banker's eyes and said a prayer. He stood up and rushed out of the bank. Outside, the ever-growing crowd pressed against him, almost stifling him. Coming hard and fast, questions hit from all sides.

"Did they get all our money?" shouted one man.

"I heard they shot banker Ozgood," yelled another. "Is he dead?

The marshal fought to get some breathing room, but he could not get through the mass of people. In desperation, he pulled his six-gun and fired twice in the air. "This is Marshal Stevens," he screamed. "Open up and let me get by or I swear I will shoot somebody." As if on command the crowd shut up. You would've thought it was Moses commanding the Red Sea to part. Folks stepped back and a small aisle opened in the frantic bunch. Fearing his path would close before he could make it all the way, Marshal Stevens hurried along the passageway. When he made it through, he headed for his office.

Staggering inside, he dropped into his chair like a sack of potatoes falling off a produce wagon. Sitting in silence, he realized his pistol still hung from his hand. Trembling, he placed it on the desk.

*****

Lonnie Youngblood opened his eyes. Lightning bolts and flashing stars soared through his vision. Wincing, he shut his eyes. His head hurt like he'd been kicked by an ornery mule. Keeping his eyes closed and lying still, Lonnie tried to remember what occurred. He had been standing in front of the saloon watching all the fun when something happened to him. That's all he could remember. He tried to rise but nausea enveloped him and he fell back into his bed.

Hearing Lonnie thrash about, the doctor approached him. "Whoa there, son," he said. "I'm Dr. Mullins. You've got a nasty gash on the

60

right side of your head. It isn't deep but I'm sure it is painful. You have to lie there and be still for a couple of days."

Lonnie tried to speak, but it sounded like a bullfrog at night calling his mate.

"I'll get you a drink of water," said the doctor.

In a moment, Lonnie felt a glass upon his lips and he drank. The dryness of his lips went away and the cool beverage soothed his parched throat. He lay unmoving for a bit, gathering his thoughts. "How long have I been out, Doc?"

Dr. Mullins dug his pocket watch out of his coat pocket. "Going on thirty minutes, more or less," he said. "But don't worry. Your wound, while painful, is not life threatening. It took a bit of skin from the right side of your head, and some hair, but everything will soon grow back. You will be fine in a few days."

Lonnie digested what the doctor had to say and thought about it. He wasn't about to lay here for three days. As soon as he felt a mite better, he would be gone from this sawbone's place. A thought occurred to him. He kept his eyes closed. "Doc, are you still here?" he asked.

"I'm here, son. Do you want something?"

"Did they catch the bank robbers?"

"No, they say it was the Stockard gang. They're about the meanest bunch of outlaws in New Mexico Territory." He scratched his short white beard. "Why, I reckon they're thirty miles from her by now. Nonetheless, Marshal Stevens is gathering a posse to ride after them."

"When's he leavin'?"

"I can't say for sure, but I expect it will be in the next hour or so."

Lonnie took a deep breath and raised up to sit on the side of the bed. He thought he was going to throw up, but he got his nausea under control. He opened his eyes. Fighting back the pain he managed to keep them open. Holding his head up took tremendous effort.

"Gimme my hat and my holster."

"Oh no, you're not going anywhere," said the doctor. "Lie back down."

"If you don't do what I tell you, when I find my six-gun, I swear, I will shoot you. Now, I want my stuff!" Lonnie stood up. His legs felt like wriggling snakes, but he held his ground and didn't fall. He coughed up an immense wad of green phlegm and spit it onto the floor. Wiping his mouth, he searched for his hat and gun belt.

"Okay, okay," said the doctor. "I will give them to you, but the moment you walk out of this office I will no longer be responsible for your health." Dr. Mullins retrieved Lonnie's gear from a cabinet shelf and handed it to him.

Lonnie set his hat on his head and buckled his gun belt. He wobbled outside and tried to get his bearings. Bright sunshine assaulted his eyes. He threw his arms up and staggered backwards until he hit the wall. "Oh, Lord!" he said. "I can't see." Rubbing his closed eyes for a few seconds, Lonnie stood still. When he opened his eyes again, he did it with great care. Standing in the shade of the Dr.'s office awning, he said, "I've gotta take it easy. I have to get used to the sun."

After a few minutes, squinting his eyes Lonnie stepped out into the street. It still hurt, but the pain was bearable. He thought for a second, then walked back to the doctor's office. Opening the door, he addressed Dr. Mullins. "What do I owe you, Doc?"

"Not a blame thing. Just stay out of my office."

"Your choice, Doc." Lonnie started to leave but he had a thought. "Which way to the Marshal's office?" he asked.

"East! Now get out of here."

Lonnie started walking east, careful not to move too fast. As he moved along, his vision adjusted to the sun. The pain in his head reduced to a dull throbbing. "Even the great red Beelzebub ain't keepin' me from riding with this posse," he said.

Marshal Stevens rushed around his office gathering up gear. He pulled a yellow boy Winchester from the rifle rack and laid it on his desk. Grabbing three boxes of .44 cartridges, he set them next to the rifle. He rolled the cylinder of his .44 Colt and dropped the six-gun into its holster.

Two men entered his office, Jake Lally, his part-time deputy, and Orville Crow, who ran the general store. "They's a whole bunch of people wantin' to ride in the posse, Marshal," said Lally. "What do you want me to do?"

"I only want six men," said Marshal Stevens. "Do I need to pick them out or can you do it?"

"Uh, I probably can do it," said Crow. "Anybody special you want with you, Jim?"

Marshal Stevens stopped what he was doing and rubbed his neck. "Let me think…are the Martinez brothers in town?"

"Sure are and they already volunteered," said the deputy. "And I'm gonna go. That makes three."

"You have to watch the office, Jake. We can't leave Puerta de Luna without someone to enforce the law."

"You're right, Marshal. Okay, I'll stay, but, I sure do want to go."

Lally and Crow started out the door. Before they could get outside, a big man pushed between them and stepped inside. "I'm going with you," he said.

"Mr. Youngblood," said Marshal Stevens. "Didn't you get shot during the robbery?"

"It ain't nothin'. I've rode the rough trails for over ten years and never once took any lead. It's not right, me gettin' shot just standing around watching. I'm goin' after them owl hoots."

"I understand how you must feel, but this isn't your fight. You have no connection with the robbery."

Lonnie pointed to the right side of his head. "Here's my connection. If I don't ride with your posse, I ride alone."

"All right, Mr. Youngblood, suit yourself. We leave within the hour. We will not wait."

Lonnie mumbled something under his breath and walked outside. He asked the first person he met for directions to the general store. He got supplies for a week, including three boxes of .45 cartridges and one box of ten-gauge shotgun shells. Throwing the bag over his shoulder he proceeded to the livery where he saddled his horse and secured his supplies. Lonnie checked his cinches, mounted and headed for the marshal's office.

When he arrived, the marshal was speaking to the rest of the posse. There were seven riders including the marshal. Lonnie eyeballed the bunch. There were two Mexicans who looked like brothers. "They'll be stayers," Lonnie thought. Two more looked like working cowboys. He recognized one man as the dumpy bartender. The last rider made him shake his head. Maybe twenty years old at the most, the kid wore a two-gun rig tied down below his waist. Lonnie laughed. "You've been reading too many dime novels, younker," he said. If the kid heard him he didn't react.

"Does everyone have, at least, a week's worth of supplies and plenty of ammunition?" asked Marshal Stevens. Heads nodded. "Good, we will head west and ride as long as our supplies hold out. I'm sure most of you know this is my first posse to lead. Heck, it's my first posse ever. Has anyone here been involved with a posse before?"

"I have," said Lonnie. "Hell, I've been on both sides of a posse."

The other riders laughed. One called out. "Maybe you should lead this one since you're experienced." No one else commented. Lonnie kept silent and pointed towards Marshal Stevens.

The marshal surveyed the group. "We, pretty much, know each other, except the big man in back. His name is Lonnie Youngblood. He's a stranger who got shot during the hold-up. I reckon he has as much right as any of us to go after the Stockard gang."

One of the cowboys jerked his head around and stared at Lonnie. He leaned over and whispered to the other cowboy, who looked at Lonnie, too. Both men had odd expressions on their faces.

The marshal continued to speak. "Boys, this won't be a picnic. We may ride hard for a week and come up with nothing, or we may catch the gang and have a fight on our hands. Whatever the case, we must give our best effort trying to recover the stolen money." Marshal Stevens perused the men. "Any questions? No? Felipe Martinez, you and your brother are the best trackers here. You take the lead. Let's ride."

Chapter 3

The bank robbers rode hard for about an hour, then slowed their horses to a ground eating lope. After a while the leader, John Stockard, held up his hand, and they stopped, giving their horses a blow. Stockard dismounted and tightened his cinch.

"Damn it, Claude," he said, "Why'd you have to smoke that old man?"

Claude Stockard, John's younger brother, scratched his dirty beard. "Aw, hell, John, I thought he was reachin' for a hideout gun. I don't like to take any chances. But, I'm right sorry now that I did it." He looked like he was about to cry. "When we set up camp tonight, I'll unsaddle your horse and take care of him. Will that make you feel any better?"

"Claude, you halfwit, the only reason I put up with you is because I promised ma I would look after your worthless hide." John Stockton ran a hand down his face and took a deep breath. "Okay, you can watch after my horse tonight."

"I'm much obliged, John, thankee, thankee, thankee." Claude turned to the rider next to him and grinned. "Jimmy, my brother ain't mad at me no more." The rider just shook his head.

"How much do you think we got, John?" said a short squat man crossing his leg over his saddle and rolling a smoke.

"Well, we cleaned out the vault," said John Stockard. "It was a little ol' bank but the only one for fifty miles. I reckon we got plenty."

"When do we divvy up the money, John?" said Claude still grinning.

"Shut up, Claude," said John. "You'll be lucky if I give you anything from this haul as bad as you screwed up."

65

Claude lowered his head and kept quiet.

John Stockard stretched and climbed back aboard his mount. "We'll ride until dusk, and then we'll make camp. I expect there's a posse comin' after us but with that wet behind the ears marshal they've got I don't think they'll give us much trouble."

*****

The posse rode at a ground eating pace, anxious to overtake the robbers, but not too anxious. Some of the riders were having second thoughts. What seemed like a good idea at the time was already looking like not such a good idea. It was hot and the thick dust proved to be almost unbearable.

The bank robbers had made no effort to cover their tracks which made it easy for the Martinez brothers to follow their trail. After three hours of riding Marshal Stevens brought the posse to a halt. "I figure they have, at least, a two-hour lead," said the marshal. "There is no way we will catch them today. We will rest the horses for fifteen minutes and then proceed."

Lonnie was glad they stopped. His eyes still gave him fits, and his head felt like two pounds of sausage stuffed into a one pound sack. It hurt like hell. He stepped out of the saddle, opened his canteen and took a swig. He removed his hat and poured water into it for his horse. "Everybody needs to give their horse a taste of water," he said. "It'll help cut the dust we've been stirring up. They'll breathe easier."

"Good idea," said Marshal Stevens. "Everyone do that." Leading his horse, he walked over to where Lonnie stood. "Mr. Youngblood, you know I'm a first timer at this posse business, so I would be much obliged to you for any advice you could give me. Just speak up any time."

"Call me Lonnie," said the gunfighter. He slung his canteen back on his saddle. "You're doin' okay, so far. If I have something to say, I'll say it. Oh, one thing. I think some of our posse are not having a good time. Best you keep your eyes open."

"Thank you, Mr. Young...Lonnie. I will do that. Do you think somebody might quit?"

66

"All I'm sayin' is pay attention to your men."

Marshal Stevens looked at the posse, but he could see no sign of anyone giving up. He knew the Martinez brothers would stay until the end. The two cowboys, Mack Perkins and Herb Deal, were tough. Not being a drinking man, he knew nothing about Fats Delveccio, the bartender. Pony McCloud, the young man, was a braggart who always talked about how good he was with his two six-guns. He just might get a chance to prove himself.

The marshal allowed himself a long luxurious stretch. He climbed back in the saddle. "We will ride hard for an hour, then slow it down. As long as the trail is plain, there is no need to rush this chase." He motioned for them to take off.

*****

Just before sundown, John Stockard found a good spot to camp. There was a small spring and plenty of green grass for the horses. They stripped the saddles and bridles off their mounts, and attached hobbles allowing them to move around and eat.

"Claude," Stockard said, "round up some firewood. Don't get anything that will smoke a lot, only make a small fire just in case a posse's close behind us." He scratched his nose. "Jimmy, you help Claude. He's liable to get lost." A couple of the men snickered and then went about their business.

After a supper of beans and bacon, the men sat about the meager fire. "You know," said the chunky rider, Moe Thacker, "that's the easiest bank I ever helped rob."

"Yeah, me too," said Jimmy Smith. "I hope it was worth our time. I'm ready to divvy that money up." Heads nodded in agreement.

"We'll split it up in due time," said Stockard. "Any of you boys that don't trust me can tell me to my face. I promise you'll get what's comin' to you."

"Aw, boss," said Moe, "you know we all trust you. It's just that we're all a little anxious with a posse on our tail and we don't know how far behind they are."

"Yeah," said Stockard. "Tell you what I'll do. I'll set up a guard all night long. That ought to alleviate some of your fears. You'll each do two hours. Jimmy, you're first. Moe, your next. Then Pablo, Dallas, and Claude, your last. If you suspect something, wake me up. If they attack us, fire your rifle. Everybody understand? Okay, Jimmy, you're up. The rest of you hit the hay. We've got a long ride tomorrow."

*****

The posse found a passable camping spot just before dark. By the time they stopped, all the men were tired. As they unsaddled their horses, Marshal Stevens began to designate chores.

"Felipe, you and Juan gather some firewood." Before he could say anymore Lonnie interrupted him.

"No," he said. "No firewood and no fire. We're probably not close to the men we're chasing, but we still don't need to advertise we're here. We make a cold camp. No coffee or hot food."

"You ain't givin' the orders here," said Pony McCloud. "Marshal, I ain't doing without my coffee. Tell this saddle tramp he ain't going to tell us what to do."

"Boy," said Lonnie turning to face the kid, his right hand dropping to the grip of his pistol, "I ain't no saddle tramp. I'd just as soon shoot you as look at you. If you want to come against me you better pull iron or move your hands away from them six-shooters."

A shocked look crossed McCloud's features. His fingers twitched uncontrollably. He stood for a moment, then he raised his hands and turned away.

"One more thing," said Lonnie. "If you ever brace me again, I'll kill you. I ain't here to play games. I'm going after the sorry bastards that shot me."

"Okay that's enough," said Marshal Stevens. "We're all tired and out of sorts, but we've got a hard row ahead of us. We have to stick together." He took a deep breath and let it out slow. "You all know I'm a tenderfoot at this posse business. Mr. Youngblood is the experienced one here. I told him if he had any suggestions he could tell us."

68

Some of the posse members grumbled but no one spoke. One by one they went about setting up camp. The horses were hobbled so they couldn't go too far. The men rolled out their bedrolls and started digging through their saddle bags for food they didn't have to cook.

*****

Lonnie was the last man to settle in. He spread out his soogan, setting his saddle at the head of his place. He had a tow sack of food and other stuff. Sitting on his soogan, he rummaged around in his sack. Digging out a piece of jerky and a couple of hardtack biscuits he began to eat. Looking around at his fellow posse men, he scratched his jaw. *The Martinez brothers are here for the duration. The cowboys have been lookin' at me the whole time. I wonder if they know who I am? Tomorrow mornin' I'll confront them. The bartender is a question. Then there's that trigger-happy fool. I expect I'll have to kill him before we're done.*

Lonnie laughed. *And Marshal Stevens, he's so inept I bet somebody else has to hold his pecker while he pees.*

He began to eat his meager meal. Lost in thought, he failed to hear Marshal Stevens approaching until the marshal cleared his throat. Lonnie jerked his head in the marshal's direction. In a flash, his six-gun appeared in his hand. Recognizing who it was he holstered his pistol. "What in the hell are you doing sneaking up on me. I could have killed you."

"Shucks, I'm sorry, Lonnie. I figured you would hear me. I need to visit with you for a minute."

"Grab yourself a chunk of grass and sit. Is there a problem I need to know about?"

"Well, I need to talk to you about what happened today. It was the ruckus between you and Pony McCloud." Marshal Jim Stevens was sweating in the cool night air. "Pony is sort of a hot-headed kid, but he means well. Along with the Martinez's, his family founded Puerta de Luna. His father owns half the town. The kid's spoiled. You're the first person to call his bluff."

"I was right about no fires," Lonnie said through clenched teeth.

"I know you were, but you come on so strong. Could you do me a favor, keep yourself under control and lay off the kid?"

Lonnie smiled. "Hell, Stevens, I thought you came here to talk about somethin' important." He bit off a piece of jerky. "I'll think about it."

When the marshal was out of earshot, Lonnie spoke in low tones. "To hell with that shit." He finished his supper and laid back in his soogan.

Chapter 4

John Stockard woke up Claude before dawn and told him to start a small fire. One by one, the rest of the robbers got up and moseyed over. Claude put coffee on and sliced pork belly into a hot sizzling skillet.

"Nothing like the smell of coffee and bacon in the morning," said Thacker.

"You got that right," said Jimmy producing a tin cup. "Here, let me get some of that black stuff."

While he ate breakfast, Stockard said. "I've been thinkin' about that posse. I still don't believe we are gonna have a problem with them, but we need to make sure. Jimmy, see those big boulders piled up over yonder. When we ride out today, I want you to station yourself behind them and watch for the posse. If they don't show up by dusk come on to the hideout. If they do, fire some shots and pin them down.

"What'll I do after that?" said Jimmy.

"Shoot for about ten minutes and then hightail it towards our hideout. I reckon we're about six hours away." Stockard finished eating and laid his plate and cup down. "Claude, when you're done with your vittles, clean mine up." He took the makin's from a pocket and rolled himself a cigarette. "Moe, I want you to get some brush and follow along behind us wiping out our tracks."

70

*****

Since it was daylight, Lonnie didn't object to the posse having a fire to cook breakfast and coffee. You would have thought it was Christmas, the way the men fretted over the fire.

"I don't know how much more of this I can stand," Lonnie muttered. He didn't like coffee and he chose to eat jerky and hardtack.

When the men had finished their breakfast and saddled their horses, Marshal Stevens called them together. "Today," he said, "we are going to push a little harder than yesterday. We need to make up time on the bank robbers."

Delveccio the bartender complained. "Yesterday was hard enough. I don't know how long my horse can take it."

"Go back to town, if you don't want to go on," said Lonnie. "We don't need you holding us up. That goes the same for any of you pilgrims. If you ain't got the sand, then git."

"I agree with Mr. Youngblood," said the marshal, "if you are having second thoughts about being in this posse, go back now, not later when it might get rough." No one said anything. "Okay, give the camp a quick pick up, and then we will head out."

Lonnie glared at the two cowboys. He walked over to where they stood. "I need to talk to you boys," he said. "Let's go over yonder away from everyone else." They moved away from the center of the camp.

"This is far enough," said Lonnie.

Perkins and Deal looked at each other. They acted nervous.

"Ever since we left town, you boys have been eyeballing me. I want to know why, and you'd better not lie."

Herb Deal broke the silence. "I know who you are."

"That right?"

"You're Lonnie Youngblood from Texas. You kill people for money." Deal was sweating hard.

"You're right on both counts." Lonnie's right hand dropped to his six-gun. A move both cowboys noticed. "I've also been known to plug somebody for talking too much. Understand?" Both men liked to

71

have broken their necks bobbing their heads up and down. Lonnie turned and walked away. The men stared after him not saying a word.

*****

After three hours on the trail, the posse rode close to a big pile of boulders. A shot rang out. Mack Perkins gasped and tumbled from his saddle. Shots kept coming. The horses began to jump around as the men frantically tried to find cover. Pony McCloud turned loose of his horse and jumped behind a big tree, but not before he took a bullet in his arm. He screamed and fell covering his head.

Lonnie and Marshal Stevens found themselves behind the same pile of brush. Bullets kept flying, and they ducked low. "There's only one man shooting at us," said Lonnie.

"How can you tell?" said Marshal Stevens.

"They're all coming from one place. We've got to figure out how to get to him."

Lonnie looked over the terrain. Manzanita and mesquite trees were all over the place. Thick underbrush grew between them. Large rocks dotted the landscape. Lonnie's eyes narrowed as he formulated a plan.

"I think I can work my way around the right and come up behind the shooter. Try to keep him down with gunfire. Holler at the men to pour it on. With a little luck, I should come up on him in five minutes or so." He took off his hat and moved through the brush.

"Men, keep firing at the shooter," said Marshal Stevens. "We may not hit him but we must keep him from shooting back."

Lonnie crawled sometimes, and he bent over and ran sometimes, depending on his cover. He had said five minutes, but it seemed like an hour before he moved in behind the shooter. He could see the man crouching behind an enormous boulder. Lonnie cat footed it until he stood less than ten feet from the man. He pulled his six-gun.

"Don't move," he said, "or I'll blow your head off. Drop the rifle and your handgun. Lay down on your stomach. Put your hands where I can see 'em."

72

Caught off guard, the outlaw complied with Lonnie's orders. Lonnie walked up to him and kicked him in the ribs. He removed the robber's belt and tied his hands behind him. Using his foot, he flipped the man over on his back. The man scowled and tried to spit on his captor.

"You sorry sack of horse dung," Lonnie pulled his skinning knife. "I'm gonna need some information from you. You can make it easy, or, I swear, I will cut you up so bad your own mama wouldn't recognize you."

No shots had come from the boulder in over five minutes. "Cease fire!" yelled Marshal Stevens. He supposed Lonnie had made good his sneak up. "Men, find your horses. I believe Mr. Youngblood has got the shooter. We'll ride up but be careful."

Delveccio shouted, "Pony's been shot in the arm. I'm going to stay here and bandage him up."

"Okay," said the marshal. "Anyone else hurt?"

"Mack's dead," said Herb Deal, his voice quivering.

"Damn. We'll have to bury him after we check on the shooter. Felipe, grab Mr. Youngblood's horse and bring it with us."

The men rode around behind the boulder. Lonnie sat on a small rock next to the shooter who wasn't moving. Marshal Stevens dismounted and walked over to him.

"Is that man dead?"

"Naw, he's just playin' possum." Lonnie grinned. "I ought to have killed him, but I guess I'm gettin' soft in my old age. He told me how to get to their hideout. It's a cabin up in the hills about a six-hour ride from here."

Marshal Stevens looked down at the shooter. His bloodshot eyes were open, but he didn't move. The marshal reached down to touch him. When he did, the man squirmed. The marshal jumped back. "What on earth did you do to this man?"

"Aw, him and me and my skinnin' knife just had a little palaver. He didn't want to participate, but I persuaded him it was in his own good to work with me. Given time and enough blood he agreed. What do you want to do with him?"

"We have one man dead and one man wounded." Marshal Stevens rubbed his chin. "The dead man must be buried and I guess Pony, the wounded man, should go back to Puerta de Luna. I reckon I'll have to send someone with him. They can take the prisoner too."

Marshal Stevens had Herb Deal round up the prisoner's horse. Herb used the lariat from his rig and tied the man onto the saddle. They rode back to where the bartender and Pony McCloud were.

"How's the arm?" said Marshal Stevens.

"It hurts like hell," whined Pony. "What do you think it feels like?"

"The bullet went clean through," said Delveccio. "He didn't lose too much blood. I think he'll be able to ride."

"I'm ridin' all right," said Pony, "straight back to Puerta de Luna. I need a doctor."

Marshal Stevens removed his hat and ran a hand through his close cropped sandy hair. "Hmm," he said. "Okay, here is what we will do. Fats, I want you to take Pony back to town, but before you go, I want you to bury Mack. The rest of us will go on. Any questions?"

"Bartender," said Lonnie, "when I come back through here, there'd better be a grave. If I don't find one, I'm coming after you. You understand me?"

Delveccio's Adam's apple bobbed like a fishing cork. "Yes, sir," he squeaked out the words.

Chapter 5

The Stockard gang moved their horses through the jumble of rocks that led up to their hideout. Going was slow. The cabin stood in a remote part of the wilderness high in the back-country hills. A lean-to behind the cabin housed the horses. Tall cottonwoods dominated the area mixed in with a few mesquites. John Stockard felt the area to be almost impregnable. The gang came to a halt and dismounted.

"Boy howdy, am I glad to be here," said Dallas Strawn, a tall rawboned red-head. "I always dread the climb up to this place."

"*Si, Senor*," said Pablo Cervantes, the only Mexican in the bunch.

"I reckon we're all happy to be back," said John Stockard. "There should be grain inside the lean-to. Unsaddle and rub your horses down before you feed and water them. Claude take care of mine."

The men bunched up and headed for the lean-to.

"Claude clean my dishes," said Claude muttering. "Take care of my horse. Fix my vittles. Kiss my ass." He took off his hat and slapped it against his leg. Dust flew everywhere. "I'm damn sick of John treatin' me like I was his servant. I ain't a goin' to take it no more. I'm goin' to tell him, right now."

"Shut up, jughead," said Dallas. "You ain't gonna do no such thing. As long as John's around, you're gonna do exactly what he says, so quit your bellyachin'."

Claude snorted and said, "Someday it'll be my turn to give orders and then everything is goin' to be a lot better. You'll see, Dallas." They reached the lean-to and began to take care of their horses.

John entered the cabin. He laid his saddle bags on the wooden table and went to work getting the place ready. He started a fire in the old decrepit stove and put coffee on. "Next time I go to town," he thought, "I'm gonna have to buy a new stove. This one's about all done in."

One by one the men moseyed back to the cabin. Most of them headed straight for the coffee. "Claude," said Stockard, "when that coffee's done make another pot." Claude frowned, but he hid his face so his brother wouldn't see.

"Now that we're here," said Strawn, "when do we divvy up the dough?"

"There's no hurry," said Stockard. "We ain't goin' nowhere 'til we know if we ditched the posse. Speakin' of the posse, Moe ought to be here pretty soon. I hope he did a good job of wiping away our tracks."

Fifteen minutes later Moe Thacker showed up. "I done good, boss," he said. "That posse will never find us." He eyeballed the stove. "Say, is that coffee hot?" Grabbing a tin cup, he filled it to the brim. "I'm about all choked up with dust. This stuff is gonna taste mighty good."

"Now that we're all here, we need to post a guard," said Stockard. "I ain't takin' any chances. We change every two hours. Claude, you go first."

"Why me, John? I'm all tuckered out. Pick somebody else."

Stockard quickstepped over to his brother and slapped him so hard he knocked Claude down. "Don't you ever sass me again, you simpleminded bastard. I'll shoot you down like a dog."

"I'm sorry John," said Claude. Tears ran down his cheeks. "I'll do whatever you say, just, please, don't hit me again." He stood up and, head down, moved outside.

*****

The posse, now down to five men, rode at a steady pace. It was late afternoon, and Marshal Stevens figured it would be dark when they reached the hideout. Lonnie pulled his horse up next to the marshal. "You know it's kind of funny, marshal," he said.

"What's that?"

"It's obvious the bank robbers tried to brush away their tracks, but those Mexicans are reading their sign just like nothing was done. Them boys must be part injun."

Marshal Stevens laughed. "Their mother was Comanche. Tracking is second nature to them."

"Is that right? Well, I'll be a Dutch uncle. Say, don't we need to stop soon and talk about how we're gonna come up on that hideout. The shooter said there's too many trees and rocks there. You can't see the cabin until you're right on top of it."

76

"We can stop right now." The marshal waved for the men to hold up. The Martinez brothers dismounted and started working on their gear. Herb Deal rolled a smoke. Lonnie got off his horse and stretched. Marshal Stevens did the same.

"The robber said when we get to the foothills, it's about a ten-minute ride up to the hideout. There is a narrow trail we can follow," said Lonnie. "When we get that close, it'll probably be near dark. Maybe we should dry camp here tonight and hit them just before daylight."

"Makes sense to me," said Marshal Stevens. "Won't we make too much noise riding up there?"

"We would. That's why we'll leave the horses at the foot of the trail and walk up. It gets daylight around five o'clock. We'll get up at three-thirty and head out right away. A ten minute horse ride should make it around thirty minutes on foot."

Marshal Stevens called the men over and explained the plan. They all agreed on it and set about making camp. The horses were unsaddled and hobbled so they could take advantage of the grass in the area without getting too far away. Soogans laid out, the men sat around eating, smoking and chewing the fat. Lonnie put his bedroll next to Marshal Stevens.

Once they settled in, Lonnie began to speak, "Some things we need to discuss, Marshal."

"Go ahead Lonnie," said the marshal chewing on a piece of jerky.

"I was thinkin' about the trail. It'll be pitch dark when we get ready to start, and there ain't no way we can see that track."

"You're right. Got anything in mind?"

"I do, but I ain't too fond of the idea. We're gonna have to wait for some daylight before startin' up the trail. "It won't do us no good to head out blind. It's gonna be a helluva lot more dangerous, but I don't see no other way."

Marshal Stevens pulled the makin's out and rolled a smoke. He didn't say anything until he lit the quirly and took a couple of puffs. "I'm afraid I have to agree with you. It will be perilous, but necessary.

I'll inform the men of our change in plans. I expect they are not going to like it." He stood and walked toward the other men.

Lonnie ran a big hand down his face. "I sure can't blame 'em".

Chapter 6

Instead of getting up at three thirty, the posse started rousing out of their soogans around four. Dawn began breaking towards five. Once again, they had to do without a fire and coffee. Everyone checked the loads on their six-guns and rifles. Lonnie searched out Marshal Stevens.

"Marshal," he said, "this is how I think we should go. The Mexicans will head out first. I will be next, followed by you and the cowboy. We'll go slow and careful-like makin' as little noise as possible. By the time we reach the hideout, we should be able to see well enough."

"If we can see them," said the marshal, "odds are they can see us."

"Chance we gotta take. It's the only way. Let's get goin'."

Marshal Stevens rounded up the men and explained the plan to them. Felipe Martinez started out first. The rest followed suit. Just enough light filtered through the trees for Felipe to make out the narrow trail. The cautious tracker raised his hand in a pre-determined signal that he'd found the path. They advanced at a snail's pace.

"I hope I made the right decision," thought Lonnie. "I've always been responsible only for myself. Now I have four men trusting me to get them through this alive. I don't like it, not the least bit."

Right behind Lonnie, Marshal Stevens had similar thoughts. "I'm the man in charge, but I have put the future of this posse into the hands of a man I don't know. He seems to know what he's doing, but he also flies off the handle at nothing at all."

Marshal Stevens prayed out loud. "Lord, watch over and protect this posse. Help us complete our mission unscathed. We are in your hands, Lord. Amen."

Lonnie looked up. Dawn showered them with rays of light. Too much light, too soon. He had no idea how much farther ahead the cabin lay. They weren't going to make it in time. He picked up his pace and soon overcame Felipe.

"You done a great job leading us, *amigo*." he whispered, "but daylight is comin' too fast. I'm gonna take the lead. Stay back with your brother." Lonnie took two steps. A rifle fired. He grabbed his left arm and flung himself to the ground.

"They see us," he hollered.

The posse scattered and went to ground. Rapid shots kept coming. Marshal Stevens caught sight of the shooter peeking over a boulder. He fired his rifle sending shards of rock into the man's face.

"My eyes! I can't see! I can't see!" the outlaw screamed and started hopping around.

Lonnie shucked his .45 and shot him down.

*****

Confusion hit the men in the cabin. They jumped up and scrambled for their guns. John Stockard yelled, "Settle down damnit. We're safe in here. Somebody look through the window and see if Moe is okay."

Dallas Strawn pulled back the corner of a rawhide flap and peeked outside. "Moe's done for. His head is covered with blood. Shit, I never thought they would find us. What are we gonna do, John?"

"Calm down," said Stockard holding up his hands. "There ain't no way them posse fools can get inside here. We've got plenty ammunition to hold them off. We've got food, water. We'll be okay."

"We don't know how many men are out there," said Claude. "I'm scared, John."

"Shut up, Claude, you idiot. If you open your mouth again, I'll shoot you, or, maybe, send you outside. Boys, gather up your weapons and ammunition, and hunker down next to a window so you can shoot quick like if need be. They're not firing, which means they're probably trying to figure out how to attack us."

*****

Marshal Stevens crawled up next to Lonnie. "Are you hurt?" he said.

"Got me in the arm. The bullet grazed me. I'll be okay if I can stop the bleeding."

The marshal unbuttoned his left sleeve and ripped off a long strip. "Turn over on your back, Lonnie. I'll wrap your arm." Lonnie flipped over and lay flat. The marshal inspected the wound. Finding that it hadn't bled too much, Marshal Stevens wrapped the arm. He tied the knot tight and sat back

"That will have to do for now," he said. "What do we do?"

Lonnie breathed deep and let his breath out slow. "Get everybody over here. I don't think they can see us, or they'd be firin'. The one we captured said a pole barn stood out back. One of us needs to belly around behind the cabin and turn those horses loose. That ought to cause a bunch of confusion inside. We need to try and panic them to come outside to fire at us or surrender."

"I prefer surrender," said Marshal Stevens.

"I prefer to blow them all to bloody hell," said Lonnie.

The marshal crawled around to every man, and one by one, they converged on Lonnie's position. Lonnie explained his plan to them.

"Since it's my idea," said Lonnie, "I'll be the one to do it."

"That is not going to happen," said the marshal. Lonnie started to protest. "You have been wounded and you've lost some blood. Someone else must go."

The Martinez brothers raised their hands.

"I'm the one to go," said Herb Deal. "I'm the wrangler out at the ranch so all I do is work with horses. I can get up there and keep those horses calm."

"The chore is yours," said Marshal Stevens. "Set those horses loose one at a time, then check the house for a back door. If there is one,

80

stay there and cover it. I think turning the horses loose will confuse them and they might surrender."

Chapter 7

While Herb Deal crept around the cabin, Marshal Stevens spoke to the men. "We will give Herb ten minutes then we'll start firing. When I give the signal, start shooting at the windows. Keep up steady fire until I tell you to stop. Now, go back to your previous positions."

Lonnie rolled onto his back and stretched his cramping legs. "I wish to hell we had us some dynamite," he said. "That would take care of them boys."

Marshal Stevens frowned. "We don't want to blow them to bits. We need to capture as many of them alive as we can. Besides, we don't want to blow the money up."

"Speak for yourself," said Lonnie. "I told you awhile ago what I wanted to do. My sentiments ain't changed a bit. I owe them for shootin' me in the head. Now I owe them more for wingin' me. I don't give a hang about the money."

Ten minutes passed. Marshal Stevens waved his hand for the posse to commence firing. A deluge of shots pounded the cabin windows.

*****

"They're shootin' at us," hollered Claude in a whiny voice.

A bullet caught Cervantes in the neck and he went down.

"For God's sake, get away from the windows," yelled Stockard. "Dallas, check on Pablo."

The outlaw crawled across the floor. He looked the wounded man over. "He got it in the neck, but he's still alive," said Dallas. "He's bleeding pretty good. I'll try to stop it with my bandanna." Dallas wrapped the wound as best he could and scuttled against the wall out of rifle fire.

Deal untied the horses one at a time and shooed them away from the picket rope. When he finished, he crept closer to the back of the house. A backdoor stood in the middle of the rear wall. As per instructions, he waited there. Just in case, he pulled his six-shooter and checked it for loads. Five rounds filled the chambers.

"We've got to get out of here. They're shootin' this cabin all to hell," said Stockard. "Dallas, go out the back door and check on the horses. I have an idea about how to create a diversion. It might keep them occupied long enough for us to escape."

Dallas opened the back door and stepped outside. He spied Herb Deal. At the same moment, Herb saw him. Dallas went for his six-gun, but Deal already had his pistol out. He emptied it at the outlaw. Two slugs splintered the doorframe. Three pounded into Dallas' chest throwing him backwards through the open door.

"What the devil!" hollered Stockard.

"Lordy, they got Dallas," said Claude.

"Looks like it's just me and you, little brother," said Stockard.

"What about Pablo? He's still alive."

"I don't think he's gonna make it." Stockard walked over to Pablo, looked down and shot him twice in the chest. "Come over here Claude. I've got somethin' for you to do. You're gonna create a diversion so I can escape."

"What do you mean, John? I don't understand."

"It's simple, stupid. You're gonna run out the front door and draw their fire, while I go out the back door."

"I can't do that. I might get killed."

"That's the chance you've got to take. Now come over here next to the door. I'll open it and you run out."

Claude stood silent, then stepped back. "Okay, John, whatever you say," he said. "Turn around and grab the door handle. Jump back when you open it so you won't get hurt."

John Stockard smiled. "That's more like it," he said. He turned his back to Claude and took hold of the door handle.

82

Claude pulled his pistol and shot John Stockard twice in the back. Disbelief covered the big outlaw's face as he banged against the door and slid to the floor with his final breath.

"That's the last time you'll be mean to me, John," said Claude. "I done took all I could." He stepped over to the corpse and emptied his six-shooter into it.

Outside, Marshal Stevens raised his hand to stop the shooting. "They haven't answered our fire in a while," he said. "I wonder what's up?

"We haven't heard from Deal," said Lonnie. "I hope he got the job done."

"Yeah," said the marshal, "me, too." He ran a finger under his nose, contemplating their next move.

The door of the cabin opened. "Hold your fire. I'm the only one alive in here. I'm comin' out. Don't shoot me now. I'm throwin' out my six-shooter." A pistol flew out the door. Claude followed it with his hands in the air.

Chapter 8

Marshal Stevens surveyed the carnage. Two outlaws dead inside the cabin, one out back. "God, what a mess," he said holding his hand to his mouth. "This is horrible."

"Horrible?" said Lonnie. "Hell, I call it justice. All the robbers are either dead or captured, and I'm bettin' your money is in those saddle bags on the table." Lonnie walked to the table, grabbed the saddle bags and turned them upside down. Wads of cash fell out and scattered all around.

"I'd say that's a pretty good haul." Lonnie dropped his hand to his six-shooter and stared at the marshal. "This money is powerful temptin'." He took in a deep breath and let it flow easy out his nostrils. "Good thing I'm an honest man." His lips spread into an evil grin.

An icy shiver shot up Marshal Stevens's spine. "I'm responsible for returning this money to the bank," he said. "Outside, you said you didn't give a hang about the money. Have you changed your mind?"

Lonnie removed his hat and ran a hand through his long hair. "Naw, I may be a lot of things, but I ain't no thief. What are we gonna do with these bodies? If we haul 'em back to town, they'll be stinkin' like all get out long before we get there."

"Good point. We'll have to bury them."

"Y'all go right ahead and do that. I ain't buryin' nobody with this banged up arm."

Felipe Martinez stepped in through the back door. "*Senor,* my brother and the cowboy are rounding up the loose horses. What do we do with these *hombres?*"

"We're gonna have to bury them," said Marshal Stevens.

"There is a stream running down the mountain behind the cabin," said Felipe. "In one spot, a large dirt bank hangs over it. It would be easy to put the bodies under the bank and cave it in on top of them."

"That's a marvelous idea, Felipe. Let's drag them out there now." He paused. "Mr. Youngblood can stay here and keep an eye on the money."

Lonnie chuckled.

"Do you suppose you can manage to stuff that cash back into the saddle bags using only one arm?" asked the marshal.

"Yup," said the big gunfighter.

A slight smile formed on the marshal's face. "Grab that body in the corner, Felipe. Herb and I will pick up John Stoddard."

*****

With the outlaws buried and their horses rounded up and saddled, the posse climbed aboard their mounts and prepared for the ride back to Puerta de Luna. Adjusting the saddle bags full of money over his pommel, Marshal Stevens pulled alongside Lonnie.

"How's the arm?"

"Okay. Felipe washed it out real good and poured some tequila on it. Burned like hell. Damn if I know how they can drink that fiery

84

stuff. I'll live 'till we get back to town and the doc can take a look at it. He sure ain't gonna be happy to see me again. We didn't exactly part company on the best of terms." He laughed.

The marshal smiled and stuck out his hand. "Lonnie Youngblood, I want to thank you for your assistance. We could not have accomplished this mission without you."

Lonnie shook his hand. "That's for damn sure," he said. Kneeing his horse, he took off down the trail. The marshal shook his head and followed behind.

BLACK-MARKET MEAT

Roberta Summers

A broad smile slashed a path through Joe Heath's hairy face. He had just swung out of Skipper's saddle when he heard the beep beep of Grant Johnson's 1935 Chevy pickup.

Joe watched over several thousand head of sheep in the Sevenmile area of Fish Lake National Forest high in the rugged mountains of South Central Utah. A canvas topped wooden wagon served as his home for the four summer months. Not easy living, but with most men out of work during the depression years, Joe was grateful for the job.

Joe hoped Grant had brought his eight-year-old son Chris, and seven-year-old daughter Becky, with him. Joe had no children of his own and had been a bachelor all of his life, but he loved kids. Grant and Delia's son and daughter were the closet he'd ever been to youngsters.

The blue pickup bumped over the last few yards of the rutted makeshift road, halting in front of the sheep camp. Delia opened the passenger door, and the children spilled out and ran to Joe. He knelt and hugged them.

Holding the kids at arm's length, he said, "You're just in time for breakfast—sourdough biscuits, mutton and coffee. How does that sound?"

Squeals of joy accompanied words of approval.

Grant reached out and shook the old sheepherder's rough, gnarled hand. "Hear there's some trouble. Missing sheep?"

Before answering, Joe tipped his stained and worn Stetson at Delia. "Yep, thought it might be wolves, or a pack of wild dogs until yesterday when I found one of my dogs dead—shot, but not before he took a chunk out of someone." Joe reached into his hip pocket and produced a bloodied scrap of red plaid flannel. "I found this in Ring's mouth. He must have torn it off his killer's shirt."

Grant took the scrap. "He killed Ring? Damn, I loved that dog, he was the best of the lot."

"Yep, buried him in that aspen grove up yonder." Joe bowed his head in a moment of remembrance. "I'll need another dog. Max can't do all that needs doin' alone. He's gettin' old."

"I'll send you Rags," Grant offered. "Hanging around the farm is making him lazy. Not enough to do. He'll love it up here. The kids'll miss him, but it'll only be till we bring the sheep down to the farm corrals in autumn."

"Rags'll do just fine. Will you and the Missus have some breakfast?"

"Thanks, but I want to go up to the summer camp and talk to Dad about this. He'll need to know. Will you look after Chris and Becky? We'll be back in a couple of hours."

"Yep, take your time." Joe hoisted Becky into the wagon. Chris scrambled after them.

Joe's wagon housed a bed, drop down table, benches with hinges to access storage space underneath and a miniature wood-burning stove for heat and cooking. Joe poured coffee into tin cups halfway up and added canned milk. He pried the lid off a can of raw honey and put it on the table for the kids to help themselves. The result was more confection than caffeine and the only time the children were allowed coffee.

Joe slapped a dollop of mutton grease into a baking pan and scooped sourdough out of a crock into the pan. "These will be done in no time." He went out and lowered a white flour sack from a high branch in an aspen tree. Retrieving a haunch of mutton, he placed it on his makeshift outdoor table and cut strips from it with a Bowie knife.

Soon the mutton sizzled in a cast iron skillet and the aroma of biscuits filled the air. "Hungry?" Joe asked the kids who said, "yes" in unison. Joe pulled out three tin plates and filled them. He lifted a bench cover and snagged a glass-covered dish filled with butter. "Here, for your biscuits."

*****

Grant honked his horn as he guided the old Chevy up to his dad's summer camp. It was a wooden framed tent house. Canvas formed the upper walls and roof which were taken down in the winter and stored. Sam Johnson stepped out onto the plank porch and waved.

"What brings you up here today? Come on inside, it's cold out here. Your mother has a fire going and a pot of coffee on." Sam shooed Delia and Grant inside the spacious one-room tent house.

"Hello Son, you're just in time for flapjacks," Annie said and greeted Delia with a smile. "Would you like coffee?"

"Sure, thanks Mama." Grant turned to his dad. "There's some trouble at Joe Heath's camp."

"What's the matter with the old geezer?" Sam asked.

"No trouble with him, but some sheep are missing and he found Ring shot dead. This was in Ring's mouth when Joe found him." Grant handed his dad the scrap of flannel.

"Shot the dog? What kind of bastard does that?" Sam turned the fabric in his hand. "Looks like a piece of sleeve, but it isn't much help. Almost everyone around these parts has a red plaid flannel shirt. We'd have to get lucky to find someone missing part of a sleeve."

"Got any ideas about where we should start looking?" asked Grant as he accepted a cup of steaming coffee from his mother.

"I hadn't thought much about it at the time, but when I was fishing over at Cold Spring Pond last week, I noticed a camp just off the trail that goes down to the pond." Sam rubbed the gray stubble on his chin. "There were two people fishing—strangers. One was wearing a red plaid shirt. They may be taking just enough sheep for food. Do we know how many are missing?"

"Hard to tell with the way sheep hide among the aspens. We won't know 'till we bring them down to the yards in the fall unless we round them up now."

"Let's go see if we can have a chat with those guys at Cold Spring." Sam swigged the last of his coffee. "Annie, put a hold on that breakfast. We're going to take a drive." Sam picked up a shotgun and a .22 rifle that were propped by the door. He handed the .22 to Grant.

"Do you know if anyone has found cattle missing?"

"No reports. Ephram Hanson's with them. They're grazing on the high pasture at the Ranch. Royce's twins are with him this summer as cowhands. When we finish here, I'll go over there and check on them."

Sam, the Patriarch of the family kept his five sons and their sons close to him. They worked his vast holdings of farms, ranches and livestock. Sam's eyes crinkled as he grinned with pleasure on hearing his grandsons worked as cowboys on the ranch.

*****

After navigating the switchbacks, Grant turned onto the rutted tracks toward Cold Spring.

A quarter of a mile down the road, Sam pointed off to the left. "There's the tent I saw."

Grant left the two-track road, easing the pickup over near the tent. He reached behind the seat and grabbed the .22 before getting out of the vehicle. "This thing loaded?" he asked his dad.

"Empty gun isn't any good. It's always loaded," Sam said. "So's this one." He patted the shotgun.

"Never thought I'd be carrying a gun just to go talk to some guys." Grant shook his head.

"Better safe than sorry." Sam called out, "Hello the tent" as they approached the campsite. No one seemed to be around. Grant ventured from the camp scanning the trees in a nearby aspen grove.

"Hey Dad, look, sheep pelts." Grant pointed his rifle toward the trees where two pelts hung over low branches.

Sam strode over to take a closer look. "They're ours. Our red paint branding is on this one. Let's see the other. On that hide too. They weren't smart about hiding evidence."

"I don't see any bags of meat hanging in the trees," said Grant.

"Neither do I." Sam cocked his head. "Someone's coming."

"Yeah, I hear laughter."

A man and woman came around a curve in the trail. "Hi there," the man called. "Can I help you? This is our camp."

"Searching for people who stole our sheep and shot our dog. You have sheep skins with our brand on them."

The campers stopped in their tracks.

"Whoa, mister. We don't know about that. We found those pelts, up yonder," said the man.

Sam and Grant exchanged looks. They didn't believe him.

"Who are you and what are you doing camping here?" Grant asked.

"I'm George Murphy, and this is my wife Karen. We hail from Provo. We're on a little vacation. We heard this was beautiful country and wanted to explore it."

Humm, city slickers. Probably wouldn't be out stealing sheep. Sam eyed their citified car parked nearby. "You say you found the pelts? Will you show us where?"

"Sure. I can show you. Honey, why don't you stay here." George handed Karen a stringer holding half a dozen rainbow trout.

"Nice looking fish," Grant commented.

"It's a good fishing hole," George replied. "Follow me. We found the pelts over on this rise."

Sam and Grant followed George up a small hill and over its crest to an open area within a copse of aspens. The stench greeted them long before they reached the scene of the crime. Sure enough, there were the mutilated heads of two sheep and their guts which had been scattered and partially eaten by scavengers. As they approached, crows and magpies complained with squawks and screeches before flying off.

"It didn't stink so bad a couple of days ago. That's when we found the pelts. We thought, they'd make good sheepskin rugs."

"You had no part in killing these sheep?" Grant doubted his story.

"Nope, but we did see three men walking to a green Jimmy truck before driving away. Maybe it was them."

"See where they went?" asked Sam.

"Nope, but I can describe them, if you want me to."

"Let's hear it," said Sam.

"They looked young, brown hair, tall and slender. Two had full beards—wore plaid shirts and Levis."

"Was one red plaid?" Grant asked. "Did you see if they had guns?

"Red plaid? Oh, yes. And the one on the passenger side let a rifle hang halfway out the window. I gave them a wide berth."

"Sounds like those Ewles brothers from Scipio. Why would they kill and skin two sheep? Food for the family? I've heard they're hard up since the old man died," said Grant.

"Not too hard up to get drunk on beer at the Canyon Honky-tonk. They're trouble looking for a place to happen." Sam backed up to get away from the smell.

A loud crack and a splintering of wood sent the men running under cover of the trees. "Son of a bitch. Someone's shooting at us," Grant said.

"We were sitting ducks. If they wanted us dead, we would've been," whispered Sam.

"Be quiet and stay low. Probably trying to scare us off."

George laid face down on the ground.

"You okay, buddy?" Grant nudged him with the toe of his boot.

George looked up and said, "Scared the crap out of me."

"Yeah, me too," Grant hunkered down next to him. "Need a hand up?"

"Not yet, still trying to collect myself. What are we goin' to do?"

"Get the hell outta here for beginners." Sam edged around the trees, staying under cover of the Aspens. Grant and George crept behind him. As soon as they reached the trail leading back to George's camp another shot hit a rock sending shards flying all directions. The three men broke into a run.

Back at his camp, George told Karen about being shot at. "Let's pack up and go home. It's not safe here."

"Probably a good idea," Sam agreed.

Karen hustled to roll up sleeping bags and put cooking utensils in a box. George began pulling up tent stakes.

"We'll stay until you're ready to leave," Grant assured them. He and Sam took up lookout posts. Guns cocked and ready.

Within minutes the Murphy's sped off leaving puffs of dust behind their maroon Dodge sedan.

Grant kicked dirt over their dying campfire to make sure it was completely out. He climbed into the truck with Sam and headed back to Joe Heath's camp.

Joe met Grant and Sam on the two-track road that led to the sheep camp. The old shepherd had both the kids mounted behind him on Skipper. Max greeted the pickup with happy barks.

Grant pulled alongside the horse.

"Glad you're back." Joe said. "Seems like more sheep are gone. We went ridin' to check on the herd. It was scattered like something spooked it. Max sniffed out blood on the ground. Looks like we lost two more sheep. Let's go on to the camp. I'll saddle Molly and take you there. Don't think the pickup'll make it."

Grant told Joe what had happened over near Cold Spring.

"I don't like it a t'all, not one bit, no siree." Joe wagged his head in disapproval as he tightened the cinch on Molly's saddle.

Sam rode Molly with the children behind him and Grant doubled up behind Joe, who led the way. With shootings going on, he didn't want to leave the kids alone at the camp. On the way, Sam and Grant discussed what they could do to protect the herd. "We need another man up here," Sam said. "Ephram Hanson's the most experienced. Go get him and move his camp from the ranch up here. With Ephram, his dog and Rags, he should have enough help until we find the culprits—leave us short at the ranch, but it can't be helped."

"Here's the spot." Joe pointed at the blood-stained ground. The grass all around was trampled.

Sam lowered Chris down. "Help your sister." He handed Becky down into Chris's waiting arms. "Go search for spent bullet shells. I want to see what sort of rifle they're using."

The law was sparse in the area. Sam wondered if he should get the county sheriff involved. The game warden might be helpful, although sheep weren't game, but if they were killing sheep, they may be poaching deer. He wondered if any of the cattlemen had lost steers since a lot of cattle grazed in the high country.

Becky and Chris placed three spent .30-30 shells in their Grandpa's hand. "No wonder there's so much blood," said Sam. "Pretty big bullets to kill sheep. More like one would use to kill deer, or cattle."

"Grant, take me back to my camp. You need to get over to the ranch and help Ephram. I'll take Delia and the kids back to town. Since Officer Jeppsen is the closest law around I'll stop by his office."

*****

As Sam mulled over who might want fresh meat, it entered his mind that the men at the CCC camp may be hungry and meat from his sheep might be going to their camp,

In 1933 the Federal Government started the Civilian Conservation Corps, the CCC, a public work relief program for jobless men. These men were put to work building roads, dams and lodges. They planted trees and did general manual work. The CCC camp in Salina, Utah, started in 1937. The men built dams for flood and erosion control. Sam hated to think they would be guilty of slaughtering his sheep, but maybe? He doubted they had guns, certainly not .30-30s, but they could buy black-market meat. He wouldn't put it above the Ewles brothers to carry out such a scheme.

*****

Sam took the children and Delia back to the farm before going to the town cop's office. After listening to Sam's story, Officer Jeppson phoned the county Sheriff in Richfield, who said he'd be there in half an hour. After that, he phoned the game warden to ask if he'd heard about anyone poaching deer.

Officer Jeppson told Sam he'd heard that one cattleman had a steer shot and the choicest cuts of meat cut off, the rest left to rot. "Sounds like someone's after meat. Seems like sheep, since they're smaller are the ones they go after most. A good cut of beef is nice, but what do you do with hundreds of pounds of beef if you don't have the means to process it?"

Sounded logical to Sam. Jeppson filled two cups with coffee and handed Sam cream and sugar. They speculated as they drank the sweetened beverage while they waited.

"I think our plan of action should be to go check out the dead steer and then talk to the men at the CCC camp. We can't do that until they come back from the dam project they're working on up near Gooseberry. If they are buying meat, they'll be able to give us a description of the men," the cop said.

"That won't be so easy if it's the CCC men who are guilty."

"I don't see how they'd have the means, the guns, the vehicle."

"I see your point, and they don't know the country. They're from all over."

When Sheriff Poulson arrived, Sam brought him up-to-date on the events, the facts and their suspicions. The group caravanned to the Mattson spread to check out the mutilated steer.

"Jeeze, what a waste," Poulson said. "They only took about fifty or sixty pounds of meat. The scavengers will eat their fill, so I guess it isn't a total waste."

"If I figure six dollars per hundred pounds, and I guesstimate that steer weighed in around 1,600 pounds, it represents a loss of about

94

$100. Can't afford many losses like that." Mattson took off his worn felt hat and ran his fingers through his thick silver hair. "We need to find these renegades."

"I'm down four sheep, probably more," Sam said. "I'm ready to do whatever it takes."

"Yesterday, I heard gossip about someone who bragged about shooting a young doe," the sheriff said. "I don't think the game warden would know where to look in the million plus acres of Fish Lake Forest for the carcass, but I'll ask him to follow up on the rumor."

Sam continued on up to his camp while the rest of the men headed back to town. "I've got to wait until the CCC men are back from their job to question them," said Jeppson.

"I want to go with you," said Sheriff Poulson.

*****

Sam stopped by Joe Heath's camp to see if there were any more missing sheep. Everything seemed to be okay. "By tomorrow, Ephram Hanson will be here," he assured Heath before going to his camp. He hated to leave Annie alone with criminals in the area. After stomping dirt off his work boots, he opened the door. "Sure smells good in here, and I haven't eaten all day."

Annie told him to have a chair and then dished up an enameled metal plate full of hearty lamb stew. "I still have flapjacks left over from breakfast. I'll warm them and you can have them with syrup for dessert."

Despite his concerns, Sam smiled his contentment. *Annie never misses a chance to feed her men.* He filled her in on the events of the day. Annie sat, hands folded and listened to her man.

*****

As soon as Grant finished helping Ephram set up camp, he headed for Salina. He needed to go to the farm to pick up the sheepdog, Rags. He knew the kids would put up a fuss. Maybe he'd find them a pup. There was always a litter somewhere around the valley.

Grant was eager for a hot bath and clean clothes. One of the luxuries of the farmhouse was indoor plumbing, a large claw footed tub and plenty of hot water from their own well— hard water, but it was wet and welcome. He sighed as he lowered himself into the tub, but instead of relaxing, his mind buzzed with angry, vengeful thoughts, replacing the grief he felt about losing his favorite dog. He lathered up, rinsed, climbed out and toweled himself dry.

Delia, called out, "Five minutes until dinnertime."

Within three minutes, in fresh overalls and a clean shirt, Grant slid into his chair at the table. "I can't wait to get my hands on the sumbitch that shot my dog."

"Grant. No swearing in front of the children."

Becky and Chris stared at their dad.

"I'm taking Rags up to Joe Heath to help with the sheep."

Becky's eyes shone with unshed tears. Chris twisted his fork, staring intently at his food.

"Sorry kids. I'll try to find a puppy to take his place."

"Oh Grant, not a puppy." Delia sighed.

"Maa-maa," wailed both children.

Practical Becky said, "We'll need a puppy to replace Rags and I'll feed him and take care of him."

"I'll help too," said Chris.

"So that settles it. I'll try to find a puppy," said Grant.

Delia threw up her hands. "I knew I'd lose that one."

Grant put Rags in the passenger seat of the pickup and headed for Jeppson's office. His mission was two-fold; find out if there was any information about the missing livestock and see if Jeppson knew about any new litters of puppies. The town cop kept a finger on the pulse of the town and pretty much knew everything that happened.

Officer Jeppson filled Grant in on the information he got from the CCC men. They had been buying meat. "It was difficult prying the information out of them. They suspected it was either black-market or stolen meat. One broke ranks and said they'd been pooling some of their money to buy the meat. It was a welcome break from their usual fare of beans, rice and bread. The description they gave was similar to what you told me the campers gave you." He added that Poulson didn't think the

96

CCC men could afford to pay for all the meat that four sheep, maybe a deer and the steer provided. Someone else must be buying the black-market meat.

After Jeppson finished his report, he said he was going up to Joe Heath's camp with the sheriff to find out what the sheepherder has to say.

"I'll see you there later. By the way, you don't happen to know if anyone has puppies available?"

"Funny you should ask. My next-door neighbor told me just this morning their pups are weaned and ready to go, but they're pricey. "

"How pricey?"

"A hundred bucks."

Grant whistled through his teeth. "Yep, that's pricey. Purebreds?"

"Yep, from registered Border Collies."

"I'll drop by and take a look." Grant went to the bank and withdrew out a hundred dollars. It took him all of five minutes with the puppies to pick one out.

Grant forked over five twenty-dollar bills and cradled the pup in his arms. He held it on his lap all the way home.

The pup did the trick. No more pouting about Rags going to the sheep herd. As Grant left, he heard Delia say, "It will be your responsibility to feed, water and clean up after him."

"We will Mama, and we'll call him Lad."

"He'll need brushing every day," she continued knowing full well from past experience, that the brunt of the puppy rearing and training would fall on her shoulders. "...and don't hold him so tight, Becky, you'll smother him." She bustled off to find an old blanket for Lad's bed. "I don't want that dog sleeping with you, hear?"

Grant whistled as he drove to Joe's camp to deliver Rags knowing he'd made his children happy. He reached over and petted Rags. "You'll be glad to be back tending sheep."

The dog's tongue lolled out after he gave a single bark and before putting his head out of the open window. The wind flattened his ears against his head.

Poulson and Jeppson were already at the sheep camp talking to Joe when Grant arrived.

Earlier, Ephram had saddled up, put his rifle in its scabbard and took off with the dogs to check on the sheep.

"Taking a rifle?" Joe lifted his brow in question.

"Not taking any chances with rustlers out there," Ephram clicked his tongue signaling his horse to go.

There had been no further reports of missing livestock. However, Sheriff Poulson had a phone call from the owner of the Canyon Honky-tonk complaining about the Ewles brothers getting drunk and starting a fight. He said they were spending money like it grew on trees. "I was about to phone you even though it was late, to get you to come and arrest them," the bar owner said.

"Those bums never had two cents to rub together. It looks suspicious. Where are they getting that kind of spending money?" Poulson asked Grant.

"From selling black market meat, but can anything be proved?"

"Not unless we catch them with the meat or in the act. We're going to check around the grocery stores to see if they're renting out freezer space. I don't have jurisdiction in Millard County where those boys live, but I'll contact the Sheriff there and get him to investigate."

Late the next day, the Millard County Sheriff phoned Poulson telling him, he'd discovered large stores of meat in the Ewles ice house. Mrs. Ewles knew her sons were up to no good and was cooperative. She hadn't seen her sons for a few days and didn't know where they were. "She looked bad. Circles under her eyes. Looked like she hadn't been sleeping. Those boys are a worry to her," the Sheriff added.

The Ewles family income was primarily from harvesting ice in the winter, putting it down in their root cellar and covering it with straw. They sold it in the summertime. It looked like they were selling stolen meat along with the ice. The boy's dad had passed away three years ago.

Having lost their rudder and disciplinarian, they ran wild. It appeared to the sheriff that Mrs. Ewles was at her wit's end with her sons.

*****

Grant, Sheriff Poulson and Officer Jeppson sat on rocks and tree stumps drinking Joe's sheepherder coffee. The men plotted their next move, but before they could formulate a plan, gunshots rang out.

"Holy shit. What was that?" Poulson leaped to his feet sending coffee flying.

"Gunfire," Heath said.

"Let's get out there." Grant sprang into Skipper's saddle. Jeppson climbed up behind him.

Sheriff Poulson mounted Molly, and they galloped off in the direction of the shots. By the time they arrived, a green pickup bounced over the rough ground making a getaway. The dogs had a man down on the ground.

"Call your dogs off," the Ewles boy yelled. "Get 'em off me."

"Ephram has been shot in the arm." Jeppson slid off the horse and ran to help him. Blood leaked between Ephram's fingers where he pressed on the wound.

Grant called the dogs off the young man. Officer Poulson cuffed him. Grant spurred his horse and took off after the truck. Poulson leaped back on Molly and galloped after him.

The driver sped over wild flowers and through sage brush careening over the rocky terrain until the truck high centered on a boulder. It stopped with two wheels spinning uselessly in mid-air. The youngest Ewles brother got out brandishing a rifle. The sheriff, some distance behind Grant fired a shot that pinged off the pickup. The surprised young man spun giving Grant the opportunity to kick the gun from his hands. He dismounted and punched the boy knocking him off his feet.

The driver abandoned his vehicle. He ran for cover in a nearby stand of aspens with Sheriff Poulson's horse chewing up the distance between them.

"Stop right there. Hands up or I'll shoot."

The Ewles boy stopped dead. He turned, fear etched his face. He closed his eyes preparing for the worst. Poulson dismounted, lariat in hand, pulled the boy's hands behind him and tied them. He remounted, wrapped the lariat around the saddle horn and pulled the young man behind the horse.

Grant strode over to the Sheriff. "Looks like you'll have a full jailhouse tonight."

"Yep," he replied. "The CCC men will miss their fresh meat, but Mrs. Ewels will know where her sons are."

THE CATTLEMEN'S GAVEL

Gloria O'Shields

"You ready yet?" Margie's husband's voice dripped with impatience.

"Be there in a minute, Jack," she answered from the bedroom. "I can't find one of my walking shoes. I think Rowdy must have taken it." Arms crossed, she stared at the golden retriever sprawled on the floor by the bed. "Cough it up. Where did you put it?" The dog covered his nose with one paw and turned his head away from her. "I don't have time to mess with you, Rowdy. Gramps is waiting in the car for Jack and me. He wants to get to the swap meet before everything is picked over." She tapped a bare foot. "Okay, but you remember, that shoe better be right here when I get back." Margie settled for a pair of flip-flops and slapped on some sunscreen before scurrying to join her husband and father-in-law.

Ten minutes later the trio arrived at the Sundown Drive-in Theater. Aside from a flock of pigeons roosting along the top of the graying movie screen, the only action the place saw nowadays was a throng of weekend shoppers.

An azure sky capped the New Mexico morning as the little group ambled from booth to booth. Gramps was a shrewd bargainer, serious about finding the best buys. Margie used to wonder why her father-in-law haunted this place every weekend. He had plenty of money and didn't need to make second-hand purchases. She concluded the excursions were actually social occasions, and good exercise for the spry seventy-year-old.

"Get a look at those pruning shears." Gramps pointed to a box spilling over with rusty tools. "I'll bet I can get those for a song," he whispered to Jack.

"You don't need those, Dad. You've got brand new shears at home." Knowing his father would buy them anyway, Jack turned toward Margie and rolled his eyes.

After two hours, the three had perused most of the booths and Margie's feet were killing her. The space between her toes was raw from the grating of her rubber flip-flops. *Why can't we just go home?*

As they approached what looked like the leftovers of an estate sale, a flash of light pierced Margie's eyes. Curiosity forced her to investigate. Sunlight had refracted off the gold presentation band on a rosewood gavel nestled amid faded, brown tissue paper in a rectangular box.

She picked up the box and took a closer look. The frayed corners of the cardboard container suggested it was the original box, but the gavel appeared unused. Holding the mallet she turned it over several times. No scratches marred the engraved inscription or the lacquered finish of the exquisite object. She was certain a similar new one would cost a pretty penny.

"How much do you want for this?" she blurted, the words escaping before she could stop them.

The vendor gave her a quick glance. "Fifteen dollars."

Years of watching her father-in-law had taught her the drill. "I'll give you six."

"Six?" The vendor's eyes narrowed. "You can't be serious?"

"Well, I don't really need it. So, if you won't come down, I'll pass." Margie turned to walk away.

"Wait...wait a minute. How about eight?"

"Sold." She took a crumpled five and three ones from her pocket and handed them to the seller.

*****

Late that afternoon, Margie eased into an old wicker chair on her back porch. The skin between her toes stung as she lowered her feet into a basin of warm water laced with Epsom salts. The intoxicating fragrance of lilac blossoms and the twitter of a tiny wren perched in a cottonwood tree failed to distract her attention from the pain.

Woof. Rowdy dropped her missing walking shoe next to the chair.

"So you did have it." She patted the dog's head and could have sworn he smiled at her.

Her morning's purchase rested on a small table beside the chair. She picked up the timeworn box, removed the top, and lifted out the gavel. In elegant engraving, the name Phineas J. Talmadge could be seen on its golden band. The remaining inscription revealed he was president of something called the Cattlemen's Association in 1945.

Wow, over seventy years ago. Margie examined the gavel one more time. *Phineas J. Talmadge, that's an interesting name.* She tried to imagine what he might look like. *Lean and angular? Husky and muscular? Did he have a beard?* Images from reruns of old TV western shows popped into her mind. It only took a moment to dismiss the possibility of a crusty Gabby Hayes look-alike. Finally, she settled on a middle-aged Hopalong Cassidy.

She rolled the gavel over and over by its handle admiring the craftsmanship. Giving her palm a slight tap with the head of the mallet she noticed the shaft was a little loose. *I'll have to remember to fix this.* She leaned back in the chair, inhaled the cool fragrant air, and wiggled her toes in the warm water.

*****

103

Margie knew the gavel was a ridiculous purchase—one of those things you buy because you know it's worth something, but haven't the slightest idea what you're going to do with it. Still, there was something enticing about the presentation piece. She put its old box in the back of a desk drawer and placed the shiny rosewood mallet on her desktop as a reminder to think before impulse buying.

Each time she looked at the gavel and read "Phineas J. Talmadge," an unrelenting urge to know about the man possessed her. *Who was he?* One afternoon, no longer able to resist, she sat at her desk and did a *Google* search. Nothing turned up under his name, so she tried "Cattlemen's Association."

"Wouldn't you know it," Margie grumbled under her breath, "There's a Cattlemen's Association in every western state."

She conducted a meticulous search checking for past presidents of each association listed on the Internet. In Texas, she hit pay dirt. The state's "Cattlemen's Association" online archives contained a thumbnail sketch of Phineas J. Talmadge along with a photograph. His weather-beaten face testified to years riding the open range. Yet, beneath the surface was the visage of a once handsome man.

Now that she had a decent starting point, Margie couldn't contain herself. An obsessive desire to know more of Phineas' story took hold. In her spare time, she scoured the Internet for information. It took months of checking and cross-checking but she unearthed enough material to bring clarity to the life of the enigma who haunted her.

*****

Born in 1890, Phineas J. Talmadge was the only child of parents who were early settlers in west Texas. He was quite bookish in his younger years and often shared with close friends his dreams of exploring fascinating far-off places. As he grew older, he developed a keen interest in the ranch business. At twenty-four, after the death of his parents, he inherited the family's large ranch. In the following years, he systematically acquired neighboring acreage and expanded the size and quality of his cattle herd. Phineas was one of the most eligible bachelors in the western part of the state, yet he led a rather solitary life. A wife and family didn't seem in his cards.

During her research, Margie uncovered information about a ninety-year-old stockman named Hank Willis who once wrangled on the Talmadge ranch. In several phone interviews, Willis helped fill-in some of the details of Phineas's life. He provided accounts of events he'd witnessed, stories heard from other wranglers, and even a few tales told by Phineas himself.

According to Willis, Clement "Clem" Murphy was elevated to foreman of the Talmadge ranch soon after Phineas took control. The following year, Clem married Amelia, a genteel woman he'd met at a church social. The couple had a daughter they named Mary. Amelia grew up in Philadelphia and was not well-suited for the rigors of ranch life. A year after Mary's birth, she took the child and left for Pennsylvania. For sixteen years a heartbroken Clem refused to agree to a divorce hoping his family would return.

On a warm summer afternoon, Clem reportedly burst into Phineas's office. Tears filled his blue eyes and his calloused hand shook as he held up a letter. In a voice brimming with excitement he shouted, "She's coming! She'll be here in two weeks."

"What are you jabbering about?" Phineas asked turning in his leather desk chair to face Clem. "Who is coming?"

"Mary. It's Mary. She's coming to live with me." Clem brushed away the tears streaming down his rugged face. He paused and his voice turned somber, "In the letter, she says my darling Amelia died two months ago."

Phineas stood and placed a hand on Clem's shoulder. "I'm sorry, my friend."

The hoop-la over Mary's impending arrival was palpable at the ranch. Clem spruced up his cabin and prepared a room for his daughter. He instructed the ranch hands to be on their best behavior around the teenager. Preparations for a party introducing Mary to neighboring ranchers got underway.

When the young woman reached the ranch, she was met by a terrible tragedy. Three days before her arrival, Clem's horse stumbled and threw him to the ground resulting in a fatal head injury.

Only seventeen, and with both parents dead, Mary was alone and far from Philadelphia. Clem was Phineas' closest confidant for many years. So, out of a sense of loyalty, Phineas made Mary his ward.

Thus, at age forty, calamity allowed Providence to shine on Phineas. Mary brought new energy into his life. Less than two years later the couple married. Despite the large difference in their ages, they were perfect for each other—sharing a love of nature, books, and a curiosity about the world. Mary's temperament was gentle and she made Phineas laugh with her lighthearted teasing. He wanted nothing more than to give her the world and share in her delight. His considerable wealth allowed them to honeymoon in Europe. They returned with art, fabrics, and china to fill the new house Phineas built for his bride.

Mary became pregnant near the end of the third year of their marriage. Awaiting the birth of his first child was the happiest time of Phineas' life. The couple spent most evenings on the porch talking about their dreams for the baby. Phineas beamed each time he caressed his wife's stomach.

Hank Willis' voice turned somber as he told Margie the next part of Phineas' story. Five months into the pregnancy Mary suffered a miscarriage. The dreadful event was made all the more heartbreaking by the loss of Mary. Complications associated with the failed pregnancy took her life one day short of her twenty-third birthday.

His precious family gone, Phineas remained on his sprawling ranch immersed in inconsolable grief. The cattle business became his solitary, all-consuming interest. In a meteoric rise, he became one of the most powerful ranchers in all of Texas.

At age fifty-five Phineas J. Talmadge was elected president of the Texas Cattlemen's Association, a position he craved. By then, it was said, grief had morphed him into a scowling irascible man. The member ranchers soon grew tired of his heavy-handed management style. Open-mindedness and personal relationships were lost somewhere along his path to domination of the regional cattle market. Phineas was not re-elected to a second term.

With age he became more and more eccentric. Ranch hands reported hearing him shouting curses as he galloped his palomino stallion across his land in the middle of the night. At seventy, he spurred too hard and was bucked off his mount landing in a nearby mud hole.

"I can't believe you didn't break any bones," Dr. Jennings scolded when he finished examining Phineas.

Later the doctor told the ranch foreman, "The old coot is too ornery for his own good. He's going to kill himself one of these days."

But, Phineas lived on.

During the last years of his life, Phineas was known to always carry a small leather satchel. His housekeeper recounted often seeing him sitting on the veranda holding the bag while engaged in animated conversations with his deceased wife. It didn't matter whether he was going to the post office, or traveling hundreds of miles, the satchel was never out of his reach.

Speculation grew concerning the contents of the bag. An acquaintance reported it contained the presidential gavel the Cattlemen's Association had given him—a symbol of the power he once wielded. His critics never doubted this story as they knew he relished control above all else.

Phineas died at age of eighty-five leaving no heirs. Mary's love of books prompted him to direct that his entire estate, valued at over ten million dollars, be sold at auction and the proceeds placed in a trust designated to build and support libraries in small Texas communities.

*****

A few days after completing her quest to find out about Phineas, Margie sat at her desk and looked at the presentation gavel. If the rancher carted it around in his satchel for years, that would explain the tattered edges of the original box. It could also explain why the rosewood mallet itself remained in pristine condition.

She remembered the loose handle and reached for the gavel. After slight twisting and pulling the shaft came out. Margie checked the head to determine how much glue she needed to securely reattach the handle. Inside she spied what looked like a wad of cotton. The packing looked unusual and aroused her interest. Using tweezers from a desk drawer, she began removing the tightly packed material. A rattling sound came from the cavity. She shook the head and heard the noise again. As she removed the last bit of cotton, she realized someone had hollowed out the wooden head and stored something inside.

"Hi, Honey. We're back from our walk," Jack called from the front door of the house.

Rowdy bounded inside. As he sped pass Margie heading toward his water dish, his swishing tail swiping the gavel out of her hand causing it to land on the tile floor with a thwack. A small yellowed piece of folded paper fell out of the gavel head followed by vivid pink, intense yellow, and icy white stones which skittered across the floor.

"Jack," Margie yelled, "grab Rowdy's collar. Make sure he doesn't eat any of this stuff." She rose to scrutinize the items on the floor. Bending down, she gathered up twenty-three exquisite stones and placed them on the desk. Taking care not to do any damage she unfolded the yellowed paper. In perfect penmanship the message said:

> *Dearest Mary,*
> *In celebration of your birthday and the impending birth of our first child, I give you one diamond for each year of your life.*
> *You, my love, are more precious to me than anything in heaven or on earth.*
> *Forever Yours,*
> *Phineas.*

Margie set the paper down and sobbed realizing Mary never received Phineas' gift.

While his critics claimed the Cattlemen's gavel reminded Phineas of the power he once wielded, Margie discovered the truth—

the gavel concealed and protected memories of the love, happiness and family Phineas lost all too soon.

LA MARCHA DE LOS MUERTOS

Anthony Bartley

The sun raged down from the flame blue New Mexican sky. Its heat battled with the air conditioner for supremacy inside the SUV's cab. Wayne's husky form slouched behind the wheel, heading north toward Gallup.

Next to him, his wife Peggy scrolled through their route on her phone's GPS app. She looked up and peered out the side window. "Not very pretty, is it?"

"A god-awful stretch of road." Wayne grunted deep in his throat—his usual annoyed response. The harsh loneliness of sagebrush, tumbleweeds and barbwire fences assaulted his senses. Sandstone plateaus and craggy arroyos sculpted snake patterns in the terrain. Crumbling mesas and desiccated plants riddled the dry earth. The word "forlorn" came into his mind.

Thankfully, traffic was non-existent. The thought of a head-on collision with some idiot checking his text messages caused a shiver to run down his spine. *No one would get to us for who-knows-how-long.*

110

Jesus, to be stuck out here bleeding...dying. A vision of his wife, his darling for the last ten years, broken in the seat next to him swam across his mind's eye. Wayne shivered.

He took a swig from his coffee mug and glanced at Peggy. His cranky mood melted some as he watched her twirling a long, brown lock of hair around her finger. He reached over and with his fingertips caressed the back of her neck. "Babe, how much longer before we reach any semblance of civilization?"

Peggy turned her attention back to her phone. "The GPS says it's about ninety miles to Gallup." She leaned her slender form toward him, placing her hand on his leg.

A low rumbling thunder shuddered through the SUV. A bright crack of lightning ripped down from the heavens, striking somewhere in the distance before them.

"What the hell?" Wayne grimaced and his heartbeat raced.

The sky darkened. He looked for clouds but saw none. He turned with a puzzled look to Peggy, who was leaning forward and staring up through the windshield. The shadow had come from nowhere. A cold rain of unease washed through him.

An earthy, cellar smell filled the cab. Static buzzed on the car radio. Peggy turned it off.

"Smells kinda wet, but—" Peggy indicated the dry landscape with her thumb.

"I don't know what happened, babe. Only in New Mexico, I swear. Every time I travel through this state something weird happens."

The sky brightened.

The vista scrolled past but the scenery changed little until a sun-bleached sign loomed on the right.

Wayne squinted. "What's that say? I can't quite make it out."

"Mmmmm, looks like an old town sign." Peggy read, "Pueblo Escondido. The rest is too faded."

"I thought you said there wasn't another town until Gallup."

"No, there are a few small ones, but I don't see this place on the map. Probably too small."

Wayne drank the last bit of his coffee. "Well, I hope they at least have someplace with hot java."

"You and your coffee addiction." Peggy patted his arm.

He shrugged and grinned. "Just gotta have it, baby." He rubbed his pot-belly. "This don't run on decaf."

Peggy rolled her eyes. "You're a dork."

On the horizon, the boxy forms of buildings appeared within a mirage-like shimmer. As the couple drew closer, they saw a figure ambling along the side of the road toward the town. His straw cowboy hat, gray pants, and shirt fit the rustic New Mexican environment. He appeared preoccupied with something in front of him. As their vehicle approached, Wayne and Peggy realized the old man walked two large-headed, skeleton marionettes. The man glanced behind as the couple approached and followed their progress. The shaggy tufts of his gray hair and his long white beard fluttered as they passed. The tailwind blew the hat crooked on his head.

Wayne watched the man's image recede in the rearview mirror. "I'm surprised you weren't taking pictures of the old coot as we passed."

"That's because they would blur," Peggy said.

"I coulda slowed down, you know?"

"Well then, why don't you be a gentleman and turn around so I can snap one of the puppet-man?" She pulled the camera case from the floor.

"Just get it when he's in town."

Peggy stuck her tongue out at him.

Smiling, Wayne squeezed her leg.

She slapped his hand as it advanced higher on her thigh.

A sudden bump and change in tire noise startled Wayne. He braked, and the car fishtailed. The pavement had become dirt. Dust billowed behind them and pieces of gravel pelted the undercarriage. He grabbed the steering wheel with both hands and glowered ahead, slowing from a comfortable cruising speed to an irritating crawl.

"That's dangerous not to have some sort of sign," Peggy said.

Her husband's grunt was all she needed to hear to know he agreed. She glanced down at her phone and saw that it didn't have any signal bars. The GPS map had turned into a blank green screen with the small dot of their vehicle appearing stationary. Looking at that solitary blue dot bothered her more than it should have. When she held up the phone in an attempt to gain a bar, she noted they were nearly to Pueblo Escondito. The phone remained useless.

Wayne surveyed the area with contempt. Then something akin to dread squirmed in his chest as they rolled into the ramshackle town.

In front of the cracked brown stucco buildings were western-style boardwalks. The verandas sagged upon stripped cedar poles. Several cars, mostly older models, were parked along the wooden curbs.

The road narrowed and branched into small residential areas further into town. Wayne noticed men and women leaning in their doorways. A few townies even raised a welcoming hand as the couple passed by. What really caught his attention were the hundreds of roses hanging from wires strung above the road, down walls, windows, car antennae, and door handles.

"Must be having a festival," he said.

"Let's hurry out of here. There's something creepy about all this." Peggy bounced her knee up and down. "We can buy your coffee somewhere else. I'll just take pictures from the car." Her eyes darted left and right.

"Agreed."

Peggy took the camera from its case and adjusted the lens. She set it on her lap and let out a nervous sigh.

Wayne took her hand, comforting her with his touch.

As buildings lessened, the road became a washboard. Everything in the car rattled and clacked.

"Did we get off the main highway somehow?" Wayne's voice quavered with the vibrating car.

"I don't think so. I didn't see any exit signs. Certainly don't see any construction barrels or equipment," Peggy said.

The small, even ripples in the road soon turned into shallow ruts.

The well-engineered shocks couldn't absorb the pounding and the occupants bounced and tossed—their seatbelts cinched taut.

"This is just becoming more and more strange, Wayne, and dangerous. Turn around."

After making a slow U-turn, they headed back into town.

Upon re-entering, they saw that more people had gathered on the wooden walkways. Bystanders engaged in conversation pointed at the car as it passed. Wayne sped up and exited the town. Once again, they hit the washboard shakes then the bouncing of deep ruts, jostling him and Peggy.

"What in the hell is going on?" Wayne slapped the steering wheel.

"We have to be on the wrong road," Peggy said.

"No, we can't be." He pointed to the dash compass. "We're going south, and I haven't turned this vehicle off any bypasses, side streets, or anything else." His voice was hard, impatient. Blood throbbed through his temples. An edge of panic scraped along the walls of his brain.

"Well, something happened. Let's ask for directions."

Wayne sighed as he braked and started a three-point turn.

Peggy noticed a figure moving toward them. The bearded puppeteer moseyed along, making his marionettes dance. "Ask him." She signaled with her chin.

"Oh, he totally looks like a reliable source of information," Wayne snapped.

"It won't hurt, and…I can get that picture I wanted," Peggy said, hoping to diffuse the rising tension not only in her husband but in herself.

Wayne turned to make a snide remark about her hobby but saw his wife's elfin grin. He sniffed and made himself calm down. As the elderly puppeteer approached, Wayne rolled down the window. "Excuse me, sir, but…" he chuckled, "I think we're lost." The clicking of a camera sounded next to him.

The old man raised a hand, letting his marionette dangle. He smiled and pointed to the town.

"No, we want back on the highway."

Another click.

The man marched his marionette skeletons closer to the couple. The stringed puppets looked like two skeletal toddlers, large-headed with petite bones.

"Not lost," he said with a heavy Spanish accent.

"Umm, yeah, yeah, we are. We're trying to get on the highway and…" he stammered over his next words, "Where—where are we?"

The marionette in his hand swayed and moved in jerky angles. With the back of his forearm, he pushed up his cowboy hat. Dark, weathered skin contrasted with his long white beard. "You are in life, *amigo*."

Wayne squinted, dumbfounded.

"What's going on?" Peggy asked.

"I have no idea." Aggravation bubbled within him. He rolled up the window and punched the accelerator. A spray of dust and gravel fanned out behind them.

Peggy gasped at the sudden velocity. "What the hell, Wayne?"

"I want to leave, Peg—just get back on that boring highway."

He slowed as he entered the town limits. Townsfolk milled along the walkways and the road. Hitting some poor pedestrian was the last thing they needed.

"Why don't we stop, take a breather, and find out where we're at?" Peggy wanted out of the car. The cab had taken on the aura of a prison cell, or worse, a coffin.

"Okay," Wayne nodded. "You're probably right."

He took in a couple cleansing breaths. A trickle of shame softened his frustration while he reflected on his actions moments ago. He slowed the car then stopped in front of a store where several people congregated. After switching off the engine, he paused before opening the door. "Sorry, hon. I was an ass."

She patted her husband's arm. "I wouldn't say that. You were more on the jerk level than the ass level." Peggy opened her door as Wayne chuckled at her observation. Her shoes crunched on gravel. The air, though hot and dry, still retained a damp cellar smell.

With a smile still on his face, Wayne stepped out of the SUV and sauntered to Peggy. She winked and grabbed his hand.

A trio of men stood chatting on the boardwalk as the couple approached. Wayne's grin turned from bemusement to sheepish. "Excuse me, gentlemen. I know I'm probably going to sound like an idiot, but how do I return to the main road from here?"

A tall, full-bearded hippie sort with sad, gray eyes turned to Wayne. An open red bandana covered the top of his head. Long, blond hair hung beneath it. "You are on the main road, brother." His voice a soothing baritone.

"I mean the one to Gallup."

"You can't, man."

"Okay, so how *do* I get there?"

"Ah dude, you can't get to Gallup, Albuquerque, Santa Fe, or Arizona for that matter."

Wayne smirked and raised his free hand in utter astonishment. He looked at his wife who now stood beside him, the camera strap resting snug between her breasts. "Is there anybody in this godforsaken town who can talk some sense?"

The tall man grimaced. "I understand what you're going through," he paused and looked into their eyes, "but you can't leave, man. No matter where you turn, how fast you drive, or when you leave, you're stuck in this town."

"What kinda weirdness is going on here?" Wayne asked.

"I can dig your frustration, brother. Why don't we go in the store? You know, have a swig and wash the dust off our tongues."

"No thanks, we need to get to Gallup. Let's go, Peg."

"Babe, maybe we *should* have ourselves a drink. That's why we stopped after all." She looked at her wristwatch. "It's only one o'clock, so we can be in Gallup by three or three-thirty."

116

Wayne scowled at the two, taking in their concern. "My caffeine level is pretty low."

"Right on." The man gave him a thumbs-up and entered the store.

The couple followed him to an old-style soda fountain. They sat at the counter on swiveling stools. The tall man introduced himself as Nate, shaking hands with the couple, who gave their names.

The soda jerk walked over. "What can I getcha folks?"

"Mountain Dew, please," Wayne said, hoping it would give him enough caffeine.

The soda jerk looked to the hippie as if needing guidance.

Nate held up a hand in a calming gesture. "They make specialized drinks here. Can I offer a suggestion?"

"What, they don't serve Mountain Dew?"

"They're a little behind the times. How about a cherry phosphate Coke with a scoop of vanilla ice cream?"

Wayne started to say something, but Peggy interrupted. "That sounds wonderful. We'll take two."

"Make it three, brother," Nate said.

Wayne gave his customary grunt.

Peggy gave her elfin grin and winked. "It'll be good."

Wayne turned his attention to Nate. "So, what's this about being trapped in town? There's only one damn road? How'd we get off the highway and not know it?"

When the soda jerk handed Nate his drink, he cupped it in both hands. "I don't understand it myself." He hung his head. "All I can tell you is every one of us here have tried to vamoose. Brother, I've tried to drive out, walk out—hell, I even tried to ride a donkey out."

An elbow bumped Wayne's arm. Peggy pointed at the elderly puppeteer walking in. "Your buddy is here."

"That guy's senile." Wayne shook his head.

"Naw, man, he's sharp as a tack," Nate said.

"I don't know. I tried talking to him about how to get out and he said 'that's life' or something along those lines."

"Yep, sounds about right. That dude, Mateo, was the first person I saw when I came to this place years ago, walking around with his two skeleton buddies."

Wayne glanced at his wife, who also had a surprised look.

"Wait, you also saw him on your way in?" Wayne stopped when the old man meandered up.

"You find a way out, *amigo*?" Mateo said, laughing.

Wayne grinned through gritted teeth.

"For one to leave," the puppeteer continued, "one must die, as one must always die." Mateo lifted his marionettes and made them dance in mid-air. The clickety-clack of childlike bones matched the rhythm of the old man's "dee-da-dee-da" tune.

Hairs on the back of Wayne's neck stood up. "It's time to go, Peg." To him, the dull yellow bones looked authentic.

*****

Wayne headed north on the main street, then turned back south, back north, down side roads, trying every direction. His eyes bulged and curses spewed from his lips. Peggy attempted to pacify his anger, but only had her feelings hurt when Wayne spouted something about her inept navigation. After a couple hours and a dozen apologies to her, he headed back into town.

More residents had come outside to prepare for the celebration. They placed roses outside their homes, others conversed with neighbors, and some carried out wooden trunks. Wayne jumped when Peggy grabbed his leg and frantically pointed to a man opening his box and withdrawing bones. She snapped a picture.

She was surprised at the assortment of the people in this village. A mixture of white, black, Hispanic, native, all mingled. She even saw an Asian woman weaving roses into a shawl. The people ranged in age from the elderly, she guessed as old as mid-eighties, to late teens. Their style of dress didn't make any sense to her either. A few wore modern looking outfits, while some appeared to be stuck in the Fifties, and others in turn-of-the-century-type clothing.

On Main Street more citizens removed bones, dark clothing, string, and long wooden poles.

Wayne leaned forward. "It must be some sort of *Dia de los Muertos* celebration."

"Agreed." Mesmerized by the event, Peggy held her camera ready.

They drove to the store hoping Nate would be there. Mateo, however, sat on the steps with his puppets lying on either side of him. He smiled at the couple as they stepped onto the boardwalk.

"Is something funny?" Wayne glared at Mateo.

"*La fiesta* is about to begin, *amigo*," the old man said.

"Yeah, whatever," Wayne marched to the store.

The couple stood in the doorway, searching the small area for the only other familiar face. Wayne grunted while Peggy tapped her toe. Nate was absent.

"It figures he wouldn't be here." Wayne snorted at his bad luck.

"We can search for him or talk to other people. It's not as if we're getting out of here anytime soon."

Wayne hung his head and slumped his shoulders. "My God, Peg. What the hell? How are we *not* leaving?"

"I don't know. Maybe this is the Bermuda Triangle of New Mexico." Her voice held a spark of humor. "It's the Albuquerque Rectangle." She hoped to defuse her husband's bomb of rage from exploding.

"It's possible." He half-smiled and rubbed his eyes with a thumb and forefinger. He appreciated Peggy's attempt to lighten the mood and ease his anger, but he didn't feel anger, just defeat.

"We might as well walk around, see the festival." She reached out and grabbed his fingers.

He stood a moment, unable to comprehend his situation. *Not able to leave? How is this even possible? A person drives on the road to get out of town, but not here. Not here.*

"We'll be okay." She had caught on to his state of mind.

They stepped into the sunlight. It warmed their heads and soaked into their bodies. Mateo sat with a marionette on each knee. A familiar anger washed over Wayne upon seeing him. He started toward the puppeteer, dragging Peggy along.

"Babe, leave him alone. Let's just mellow out and see what's going on. I still have a bunch of pictures to take." Peggy led him to the dusty road.

"I think we can find out right now what's going on. It's obvious he's not telling us everything."

"Maybe he's just crazy."

"Maybe we are, too." He continued forward.

Mateo looked up and tipped his hat. "*Amigo*."

"Alright, *hombre*. I know you know what's going on. So talk."

The old man shrugged. "I know *nada*."

"Cut the crap! Tell us what we've gotten into."

The old man smiled, exposing yellow-stained teeth. "Today's *La Marcha de los Muertos*. A day of joy, *alegría*!"

"And what's that?"

"The day we *celebramos* death and remember it is only another step in life. You will understand."

"I don't want to understand. I want to drive to Gallup."

"You don't have a choice, *amigo*. You will understand one way or *otro*." Mateo stroked his beard.

Wayne's face crinkled with fury. "Goddamn it, make sense!"

"Babe, let's go." Peggy tugged on him. "He's not going to tell us anything useful."

"Maybe, I just need to knock the shit out of him."

"Come *on*." She raised her voice and tugged at her husband.

Wayne scowled at her for a moment. He saw fear in her eyes, and then the hardness in his own ebbed. Grabbing her hand and holding it, he felt its warmth and desperation. He backed away from the old man.

Mateo's face became grim. "I am sorry, *amigos*. You just got here in the single moment Pueblo Escondido is found. You are our first visitors in many years. I have no power to release you." He shrugged his shoulders.

Wayne sighed. "Unbelievable." He turned and walked away with Peggy.

The couple meandered around the town, chatting with locals. Wayne's neck and back muscles relaxed the further he moved away from the store. Distance from the strange old man seemed to ease the anxiety.

Peggy gripped his hand, letting it go only when a photo opportunity presented itself. Though the day's events had been unsettling, exhilaration came with the adventure. She enjoyed watching the people, so different in looks and mannerisms, engaged in macabre activities.

Everyone spoke little and seemed preoccupied with preparations. Some plucked petals from roses and spread them onto the street. The rosy scent wafted through the air. Others dropped petals into the wooden boxes.

They passed one Native American woman sitting cross-legged with bones piled neatly beside her. She put them together like a puzzle and tied them in place with dark pieces of string. Lifting a completed leg, the woman shook it to see if her knots held.

The couple traveled around the town, watching as people assembled skeletons, some of which still held remnants of flesh.

In some homes, larger boxes remained closed.

Peggy thumbed to the casket-like containers. "Wayne, you think those have actual bodies? You know, like with everything still intact?"

"Based on what I've seen I wouldn't doubt it."

They rounded another corner and saw Nate. He was pouring wood polish onto a rag and rubbing it on a coffin.

"Nate," Wayne called out.

"Hey, guys, how's the walkabout?" Nate looked up at the pair.

"Interesting. So, what is all this?"

"You know, preparing for the march. It's the one day we get to see those who've gone to that big party in the sky."

"You mind me asking what's in the box?"

"You'll see at the parade, brother."

"It's not a body is it?"

Nate halted his polishing. "You'll see at the *parade*."

"Okay. When does it start?"

"Dusk." Nate went back to polishing.

"We have a few hours, then."

Nate nodded and continued his work. "Yeah, dude, we have a while."

"I'll let you get back to it then."

"Wayne," Nate stopped. "Peggy. After dusk, stay together— don't leave each other's sight."

The couple regarded his warning.

Wayne cocked an eyebrow. "Okay. Seems we can't go anywhere anyway."

"I'm serious. Stick together and you both might make it through this, you dig? At the risk of sounding *loco*, as if that hasn't happened already, beware of the shadows."

"Shadows?" Wayne squinted at Nate.

"Uh-huh, ones that seem to come from outta nowhere like no one's around to cast it."

"Outta nowhere?" Wayne muttered, thinking back to when they first arrived.

"That's weird, Nate." Peggy felt her heart speed up.

"I'm tellin' ya, be on your tippy-toes and sharp-eyed, my people."

"We will," Peggy said.

As the two walked on, Nate returned to his polishing. He stopped again and tenderly traced the edge of the coffin. "See you soon."

Wayne and Peggy didn't know if he spoke to them or whoever lay in the coffin.

*****

"I say we head to the store and sit this out," Peggy took her husband's hand and leaned into him.

122

"Me too." Wayne raised her hand to his lips and kissed it.

Once at the store, Peggy placed her camera in their vehicle then went into the store where they bought cold cuts and bread. They returned to the veranda, sat down, and waited for dusk. After finishing his sandwich, Wayne wandered to the walkway's edge and gazed at the horizon. The dirt road went on until it dwindled into a thread clipped by skyline shears.

The sun hovered above the horizon, holding with it the town's mystery.

"Well," Wayne said, "should we head over to the other side of town and maybe find out what's happening?"

"Sure." Peggy smiled and put her arm around her husband's waist. She pinched a love handle.

Wayne squirmed. "Stop, you vixen." He pulled her close and kissed her on the head. His stomach fluttered when they stepped onto the road, heading toward the crowd of citizens and their strange festival.

At the center of town, a large gathering of people milled around with skeletons swinging from long poles. One man made his dance a ghoulish jig; its limbs clattering like graveyard chimes. Others set their open-lidded boxes upright on dollies and rolled them around on the road. Inside the caskets, bodies were at varying stages of decay.

Wayne grew aware of a cellar smell...*the smell of an open grave.*

The movement ceased, and the crowd turned its attention to the western horizon and the sinking sun. A timid breeze blew across the road, stirring the dust.

Peggy and Wayne watched the crowd march forward. The transformation commenced. The dimmer the sky, the more life-like the cadavers became. Shadows formed. It seemed that flesh molded upon the bones.

"My God," Wayne said.

"This is incredible." Peggy reached toward her chest as if to grab something. "Shit, you gotta be kidding me. I forgot the camera." She spun and jogged away.

Wayne stood spellbound by the transmutation. Nate's face stood out in the crowd. His open casket revealed a female cadaver with a beaded headband. Then, as if punched in the gut, Wayne recalled the warning and whirled around.

His heart heaved and pounded. *Stay together.* He sprinted after her, but like a bad dream, he couldn't achieve the speed he wanted. *Stay together.* Adrenaline forced his leg muscles to dig in and push his weight through the darkening town. *Stay together!*

He yelled her name, but his contracting lungs made his words breathless, wispy.

He glimpsed a shadow. It lurked under a tree then writhed like a curtain in the breeze. Wayne sprinted harder. The shadowy figure twisted. Ethereal fingers stretched forward, sharpening into skeletal points.

In one last desperate attempt, he cried out, "Peggy! Stop!"

She slowed and turned as Wayne barreled toward her.

"What—" Her words cut off as the shadow slithered across the ground.

Darkness seeped between them. Eyes locked. Was that an "I love you" Wayne mouthed? Peggy reached out.

Slack-faced, Wayne fell to his knees, then onto his face. His momentum causing his body to skid forward.

The scream hurt her throat. She barely noticed pebbles digging into her knees when she dropped next to her husband.

Stepping into the dying light—his shadow stretching over the couple—Mateo stood with his two marionettes.

"I was in love once, but…" he bowed his head and looked at the road. "She died giving birth. I came here with my two *bebes*, my twins. I left them in the wagon to buy corn and mutton, but I got drunk instead. Left them in the hot *Neuvo Mejico* sun. When I returned, death had taken their tiny *espiritus*, leaving only the vessels." Lifting the miniature skeletons, Mateo smiled and cradled one in each arm. "Two died, two got to leave."

Peggy closed her eyes with grief and realization. Tears spilled down her face. She sniffed and choked out, "They leave in death, but we always stay."

"*Sí.*"

She opened her eyes and watched with blurred vision as the shadows grew long, filling the town with darkness. Moonlight spread its silvery sheen upon the town.

Peggy struggled to turn Wayne over. Dust and small rocks clung to his face. She brushed them off then gazed up at Mateo. Flesh formed on his marionettes. A sound of two babies cooing. The smell of an open grave dissipated, replaced with the smell of roses.

"How is this happening?"

"It is Death's village. You would have to ask him."

"Will my husband come back?"

Mateo gave a sad smile. "Not this time, *chica.*"

The day died and the night lived. Laughing and cheering echoed in the street behind her as people danced and kissed their loved ones. Bones and corrupted flesh no longer, the dead marched with the living.

Peggy brushed Wayne's hair to the side. Tomorrow she would start building the coffin.

NAOMI, BUDDY AND ME

Linda Fredericks

F irst time I laid eyes on Naomi Lamont was August 1968. I sat on the rickety bleachers under the brush arbor of the powwow grounds. It was dusk. Long streaks of pink painted the darkening sky as I waited for Grand Entry. Soon a parade of dancers wearing buckskins, beads, feathers, moccasins, bells and shawls created a blur of colorful movement as drumbeats ushered them inside the dusty circle for the 25th Annual Heart Butte Powwow. I'd been invited to participate in the Wounded Warrior Honor Dance.

Next to me sat my nephew Oren, my oldest sister's illegitimate son. Only seven years apart in age, Oren and I grew up more like siblings than uncle and nephew. We lived in the same household for the first year of Oren's life. I thought of him as my little brother. My Aunt Lily and Uncle Leroy adopted him when he was a year old. Many people outside our family who didn't have the inside scoop, thought we were cousins. There's a strong familial resemblance we've been told; tall, dark, and handsome—cliché, but true. Though we're not brothers, in our hearts we are. As we grew up, we became closer and now whenever I'm home visiting, we hang out together.

Anyway, Naomi Lamont was a contestant in the fancy shawl dance at the powwow which she won. The contestant number she wore was 187. I remember it because it's the first three numbers on my Army dog tags. I interpreted this number connection as some kind of sign from above. And for that reason I could not take my eyes off her the entire night. Yes, she was beautiful, still is with long dark hair and amber colored, almond shaped eyes. Yep, she had a great body and still does five foot five with voluptuous curves, but her allure went beyond her looks. There was something else that attracted me to her. It was like I already knew her somehow. From some other lifetime, some other place, like a *deja vu* about her that I have come to understand as "soul recognition." There was something about Naomi Ruth Lamont that my soul recognized and I believed her soul did too.

One thing Naomi and I had in common was growing up in a small rural Indian community on the reservation. That experience connects all of us Indians regardless of tribal affiliation or geographic locale. There's a commonality among us that's difficult to explain.

While we were at the Powwow watching Naomi dance, I asked Oren if he knew her. He did. "She's Tex Lamont's daughter. Remember him?"

"Oh yeah, the famous bull rider." I had a vague recollection of her when she was a kid. But I hadn't seen her for years. After serving in Vietnam my memory wasn't what it once was. Oren said he'd gone to high school with her, said he sat next to her in American History their senior year. Said, even though he wanted to go out with her he never did. Moreover, he didn't bother to introduce me to her at the powwow that night and that, as they say, was that.

Or so I thought, until the following month when I walked into the landmark Buckhorn Bar in Laramie, Wyoming and found myself ordering a Corona with a twist from her. She looked at me with a don't-I-know-you expression. I could tell she couldn't place me.

"Where are you from?" I asked when she returned with my drink.

"Heart Butte. Do I know you?"

"We've never met if that's what you mean, but I saw you at the Heart Butte Powwow last month. You won the Fancy Shawl contest."

"Okay, I thought you looked familiar. You're Gabriel Le Beau. You were in the Honor Dance?"

"Good memory," I said. "Naomi Lamont, right?"

She nodded, smiled, and put her hand out to shake mine. "Nice to meet you, Gabriel."

"Please," I said, "call me Gabe."

Naomi was a first semester freshman at the University of Wyoming. She seemed reasonably impressed with me as a law student, a Vietnam Vet, and a folk singer and wasn't bothered by my seven-year seniority. I was impressed with her too since Oren had described her as an honor student, champion barrel racer, powwow dancer, and now a Sacajawea Scholarship recipient.

She landed a job at the Buckhorn because her famous, bull-riding dad, Tex Lamont, rode the rodeo circuit with the bar's owner, Bobby Brand. I became friends with Bobby over the three years I'd been in Laramie attending law school. I provided live music at his bar for a couple beers, free meals, and a nominal fee.

So at any rate, in what I consider the natural order of the Universe, Naomi and I started dating, fell in love and began living together. And to seal the deal I got her a puppy for her twentieth birthday. By then it was November. We went over to the Hitching Post in Cheyenne to celebrate. In the car on the way I gave her a "little gift"— a Black Hills Gold leaf necklace I bought in Denver when I was there for the Indian Child Welfare public hearing. I told her I'd give her, the "big gift" when we got back to my camper which was parked at the KOA Campground in West Laramie, and had been for the three years I'd been in Law School.

As we walked up the narrow metal steps of the landing to the front door of the Airstream, she heard the "big gift" before she saw it.

"Oh my God," she said. "You got me a puppy?"

"Yup, a beautiful little black and white Border Collie."

"Dang, Gabe. I thought my 'big gift' was a stuffed Teddy bear."

"A stuffed bear? What would make you think that?"

She shrugged her shoulders, tilting out her hands, a "who knows" expression on her face.

I pulled the door open and Naomi charged inside. The puppy yipped and scratched in a large cardboard box in the middle of the living room. I had tied a big red bow to his black braided leather collar.

Her eyes were the size of saucers. "He's beautiful. Hey, little buddy." She said as she picked him up out of the box. "What's his name?"

"Sounds like you already named him 'Buddy'."

"Yes, Buddy is the perfect name for him, innit?" She stepped toward me holding Buddy in one arm, reaching out to hug me with the other. "I love him, Gabe. What an amazing, wonderful gift, and what an amazing, wonderful birthday. Thank you."

We kissed over Buddy's head as he yelped and wiggled between us.

"Don't cry, Naomi, be happy."

"I am happy," she said. "I'm so happy. I cry when I'm happy. You should know that by now."

Naomi was real emotional. I guess that's what I liked most. She was passionate about many things; politics, the Denver Bronco's, horses, her love for me and her writing. I thought she was a gifted writer. She shared a number of stories and poems she had written especially about giving her baby away for adoption earlier that spring. I felt sorry for her loss and wanted to infuse a bit of joy and love into her life.

Nothing says love like a puppy, and Buddy was pure love. I thought the energy from a puppy would enhance the dynamic of my relationship with Naomi and I was right; it did. Buddy complimented us. He made us feel like a family, which was important to both of us.

Naomi had three younger brothers, and I had eight sisters and two brothers. Naomi had numerous aunties and uncles on both sides and so did I. Our parents' siblings had kids and their kids had kids so we both had a multitude of cousins. Naomi's brothers didn't have kids yet, but my siblings did so I had a number of nieces and nephews, too. All of it translated into one big ass extended family in which everyone had dogs, and now Naomi and I had one. Bottom line, family is important. Family is like many drum beats resonating in one's heart.

Buddy had some distinctive markings, a black spot encircling his left eye and white socks on all four feet. His eyes were soft brown and his ears, bent at the tips, had black polka dots inside and out.

Naomi and I got the biggest kick out of our little dog's antics. After having Buddy around for several weeks, Naomi said, "If I had a dollar for every time this little doggie made me laugh, I'd be a millionaire."

Buddy was whip smart and I had no trouble potty training him. All he needed was a strategically placed newspaper by the front door to understand what it was for. Within a few days he figured out that by standing on it and whimpering, one of us would open the door to let him out. He loved to steal our socks and parade up and down the hall with one or several in his mouth. He was notorious for getting tissue out of the trash baskets, chewing it up into spit wads, and depositing the little white balls all over the trailer. Finally, we snapped to what those little white balls were.

Buddy had the receptive vocabulary of a small child by the time he was six months old. We had to spell words like "cookie" and "walk" to keep him from going ape shit. Certain words caused him to dart back and forth between the living room and the bedroom, jumping on the couch, leaping over the arm and then knocking down the trashcan. If a shoe happened to be lying on the floor he'd pick it up, toss it in the air and begin the whole routine all over again. When I said the word "rest," he'd lie down on the spot, panting and slobbering. I had a knack for training him to heel, sit, stay, roll over and play dead. When he played dead, he'd stick his tongue out. Yup, he looked dead.

Naomi made time in her schedule to walk him on days when I couldn't. She often took him over to her apartment to visit her friend

Ginny and her parents who had become a part of our extended family as well.

I built him a doghouse inside an L-shaped fenced enclosure behind my trailer. He seemed to enjoy having that space while we were gone but as soon as either of us showed up he'd bark his head off until we'd bring him inside. He ate with us. He slept with us. Hell, he was like our kid.

We walked him out beyond the trailer park on the vast plains of low hilly rock formations and coulees stretching for miles toward the Laramie Mountains. Buddy romped in the tumbleweeds and tangled brush, chasing jackrabbits, sage hens and flushing out horny toads, lizards, and prairie dogs to his heart's content. On those walks we discovered, to our amazement, huge agate beds in the sandy soil of the Laramie prairie.

On Sundays we'd walk Buddy early in the morning and spend several hours collecting beautiful agate specimens of various colors and shapes. We took to putting them in a big pickle jar inside the front door. Before we knew it we had three pickle jars full.

I said, "These stones have got to be worth something." I vowed to take them to the local rock shop to have them appraised. Naomi found a huge piece of jasper. She knew what it was because her Grandma Ruth had given her a jasper necklace for her sixteenth birthday and the stones had the same striations and matching colors. For Christmas that year she made a Jasper pendent on a leather thong for me.

One Saturday morning I took the jars of agates to the rock shop over on Broadway. The owner gave me three hundred bucks for the three jars and asked if I'd bring in more. He said no one had discovered the agate beds in the area where we walked. Based on the stones we found, it was a "rich" deposit, especially for jasper, serpentine, and quartz. I saw collecting agates as an easy way to supplement our meager incomes, so I collected more often. Every few weeks I'd cash in a jar and split the loot with Naomi. I joked we ought to change Buddy's name to "Lucky."

Even though I had given Buddy to Naomi as a gift I felt Buddy was more my dog than hers. That was okay with her. We both loved that dog. He added a dimension to our lives and to our relationship that didn't exist before. He made us want to get married and have children. He was the beginning of our extended family and I wanted nothing more than to get on with it. Naomi, on the other hand, wanted us to graduate first before tying the knot which we never officially did.

*****

Buddy lived for fifteen years from 1968 to 1983. He went with us to Penn State where Naomi attended the Native American Master's Program, and I did a visiting professorship on Western Water Law at the law school there. He also went with us to Boulder for two consecutive summers when she worked on her second master's degree at the University of Colorado while I consulted at the Native American Rights Fund office in Boulder.

Buddy loved being with us but he also loved being on Naomi's folks' ranch, where he could herd cattle for which he was bred. Free to roam their vast tree lined property. Naomi's dad, Tex said, "He's the smartest doggone herdin' dog I ever seen." Buddy went with Tex and Naomi's brothers when they drove their cattle up the mountain to the summer range the last few years of his life.

Then one day in December of '83 he went missing. Tex told Naomi, "Old dogs do that. They just wander off and find a place to die in peace." She went looking for him every day for a week in the three feet of snow that covered their eighty-acre spread.

I was staying at my folks' place. My dad had suffered a stroke that nearly took his life and was unable to keep their ranch going on his own. Naomi and I had broken up earlier that year. She detested my occasional transgressions with alcohol. She never forgave me for getting drunk and disappearing for ten days after I failed the bar exam. I hadn't seen her much lately, although we talked on the phone from time to time. I missed her horribly, but she refused to stay with me while I was helping out my parents. She said she wasn't comfortable there. I didn't push the issue. Naomi was head strong and downright stubborn.

One night while staying with my folks, I was watching TV in the living room and happened to look out the front window to see her car parked in the driveway. She didn't honk or come to the door. She just sat there in the cold, snowy dark. I grabbed my fleece-lined jacket, putting it on as I went out and jumped off the front porch. I saw her through the windshield, arms crossed on the steering wheel, her head resting on them not looking in my direction. I knew something was wrong.

Opening the passenger door, I sat on the cold leather seat. "Naomi, what the hell's going on?" When I saw her face I knew it was Buddy.

She burst out crying. I reached out and gathered her in my arms.

"Buddy's gone. I went looking for him every day but I can't find him."

"Oh baby, I'm so sorry."

"I can't believe he'd just wander off."

"That's what old dogs do," I said.

"I know that's what Daddy said too, but he seemed fine."

"One thing about dogs, they know when it's their time."

"Noooo!" she wailed.

I held her tighter and kissed her cheek and neck, which made me cry too, and then I kissed her lips. We sounded like two wounded nocturnal animals howling in the night. I managed to squeak out, "Don't cry, Naomi, I got you." We bawled like two orphaned calves. Finally, she went limp in my arms. "Come on, baby," I said. "Let's go inside where it's warm."

I suppose we needed each other's touch, which we hadn't felt for some time. We made love that night with all the sweet tenderness of our first time together. We reminisced about Buddy and our lives over the fifteen years of our turbulent relationship. I speculated silently about our future. I still wanted to marry Naomi and live happily with her for the rest of our lives, but I couldn't find the words.

*****

The following summer Tex found Buddy's remains on the north-forty fence line one morning when he was out cutting hay. Naomi called to tell me. We buried what was left of him, hair and bones. I carved a headstone for his grave with a haiku Naomi had written for him.

Buddy was our dog.
God spelled backwards is dog,
A divine being.
*****

In the fall of that year Naomi began a relationship with my nephew, Oren. When that happened I went on a bender for the rest of the year. I dried out, joined AA and haven't had a drink since. After almost twenty years of being stuck in a dark abyss, I was becoming what Naomi wanted me to be: clean and sober. Turns out it's what I wanted for myself, but I didn't know it at the time.
*****

Then in the spring of 1993, before she moved to New Mexico, she came to my work at Tribal Legal Services. I happened to be sitting at my desk looking out the big picture window in my office. The dry Chinook howled down the east slope. Gigantic waves of snow like white caps flew from the jagged peaks of the Wind River's into the huge blue of the cloudless sky. The sun's reflection so bright it made my eyes water. Like a mirage I saw Naomi walking across the parking lot toward the west entrance of the building. Seeing her made me smile. Her long dark hair danced in the wind.

It was lunch hour and everyone was out of the office except me. Down the hall I heard the service bell ring at the reception counter. I knew it was Naomi. When I appeared in the doorway, she smiled.

"Hey, Gabe, I'm glad I caught you."

"You're as beautiful as ever, Naomi." I noticed she was wearing the Black Hills gold necklace I gave her for her twentieth birthday.

"Thank you, Gabe."

She was planning to trade her car in for a new one and needed my signature. She put my name on the title when she first bought it. At

134

that time she wanted me to feel like the car belonged to me too. As I signed the title I said, "You know I've been sober for eleven years now."

"Yes, I heard. That's so great. I also heard you married Linda Spotted Eagle. I'm glad you found someone, Gabe. I'm happy for you."

I looked at her and smiled. "Yeah, we have a daughter," I said. "I named her Amber after the color of your eyes." I don't know what made me say that except it was true.

Naomi put her hand over her mouth. Her eyes were like wet stones. I boosted myself up on the counter and swung my legs over landing on the other side. I gathered her in my arms and kissed the top of her head.

"Don't cry Naomi, I got you." I held her tight until she stopped shaking. I puzzled at why she had come undone. I suppose like me she realized at that moment we were never going to be married or have the children we once talked of. When I loosened my grip, she leaned back enough for us to make eye contact. I took her face in my hands and kissed her deep and slow. I looked into her eyes again. "I will always love you, Naomi."

"I know Gabe," she whispered. "I will always love you too." She smiled, pulled away, turned and walked out the door. I ran down the hall to my office. Through the big picture window, I watched her run across the parking lot to her car. She got in, backed up, and drove off.

*****

Whenever I think of that day, I close my eyes and see myself holding her for the last time and kissing her lips. I remember seeing her for the first time at the powwow then meeting her a month later at the Buckhorn Bar. I thought our lives were a predetermined destiny and in a way they have been, just not in the way I envisioned.

Sometimes I hold the piece of jasper she made into a pendent for me and I cry. When I hear or sing the song, "Girl of the North Country," I think of the three of us—Naomi, Buddy and me walking the prairie out beyond my trailer. The Laramie Mountains snowcapped against the huge blue Wyoming sky.

THE BLIZZARD

Traci HalesVass

The blizzard overtook us halfway home to our cabin above Durango, in Colorado. It had been a stressful and uncomfortable holiday dinner with my folks in northern New Mexico. Jamie tried to be good, but Mom just hammered him. She doesn't get the artist he is, and if he's not a businessman, by her definition, then he's worthless. Dad is relentless in his silent disregard for Jamie not providing for his daughter in the manner he thinks I deserve. I don't know why we go there, but we do. We can't go to Jamie's family, orphan that he is.

He was sullen on the ride home, and I bounced between trying to cheer him and defending my parents. Finally he shushed me. Actually shushed me. Then I saw why. It was a black-out, one of those storms where the snow comes at the window so fast you can't see past it, patterns and designs against a black, black background that could be beautiful, but so often become deadly. The road was a back country two-laner with no street lights. Here in these mountains the snow piles up fast.

We slid. That breathless feeling of floating completely out of control, of flying. Ethereal until the landing. Hard. The sound of silence. Tick, tick, tick went the car in the darkness of the wild.

Jamie was quiet. I asked him, "Honey, are you okay?"

He didn't answer.

Dread flooded me as I groped for him in the blackness. He wasn't where he should have been—wasn't in the driver's seat. His seatbelt was empty. His feet rested awkwardly on the steering wheel and his upper body filled a hole in the glass of the windshield. He wasn't moving.

As snow people, we carry an emergency kit. I felt my way around the back seat. The backpack was there, as welcome as a Christmas gift. I pulled it up to the front, where Jamie's legs had started thrashing. By the time I found the flashlight, he'd dragged himself halfway back into the front seat. Now a gush of frozen air whooshed inside as he sat back down, the window hole ushering in the outside.

"Jamie, are you badly hurt? Jamie, can you hear me?"

He jumped at me, grabbed my shoulders and tumbled both of us out the car door. We rolled together. He shot up, dragging me with him and marched through the snow a few feet. He didn't let go of me until he collapsed. "Jamie? What…"

A boom shattered the night. I swung the flashlight, which I miraculously still held, over to the sound. As the light hit the car, the last visible part, the driver side headlight, disappeared. "Jamie? How did you know? That snow cornice just…it would have buried us."

Shining the light back at him I saw how much blood covered his face. A gaping laceration from his ear to his lip pulsed out thick red blood.

"I don't know," he muttered. "I just don't know. But I knew we had to get out of there."

"How do you feel?"

He put his hand to his head and brought it into the light. Bloody. "I don't hurt, but I feel a little…dull or something.

Energy seemed to infuse him and he stood again, pulling me up with him. "Becca, are you in pain? Your face! You're bleeding!"

"It stings, Jamie, but not bad. Probably a few cuts from the windshield. What do we do now?"

"That way," he said and pointed toward a light flickering through the falling snow. "There."

"I think we should go back toward the highway, don't you? That would be up."

He was looking toward the light, still pointing. "No. No cars for too many hours. That way." He started trudging through the knee-deep snow, into the woods.

I had no choice but to follow with the flashlight. I managed to hold onto the backpack. As we moved through the snow, I inventoried its contents, took out a pair of gloves. "Jamie, put this on and keep your other hand in your pocket. We only have one pair of gloves. I'll put the other one on my flashlight hand."

We stopped. He held the light so it shined into the pack while I pulled out a stocking cap. "You wear this. It will help with the bleeding. I have a hoodie."

Other than a couple flashlight batteries, a book of matches and a chocolate bar, there was nothing left in the pack. Those items would be priceless later, maybe.

Trudging on I could tell Jamie was losing strength. The cuts on my face and head stung, and my shoulder was starting to hurt. The cold seemed even colder on the right side of my neck, and it bit into my nose and cheeks. Jamie stumbled and stopped. He stared straight ahead, eyes fixed on nothing I could make out.

"Do you still see the light?"

He didn't answer me. I looked in the direction he was looking. Blackness. Then a tiny pin prick of light sparked and seemed to catch, growing a little brighter. "Jamie, I see it. The light. We are getting closer."

He stood as if frozen. I shone the flashlight on him. He didn't blink. His skin under the cap was pale, almost blue. Blood crusted black around his mouth and the cut on the right side of his face. No more blood flowed though. "Jamie? Move, we've got to keep going."

The seizure started before he hit the ground, nearly burying him in the snow. I tried to keep the snow out of his face, keep his nose and open mouth clear. He thrashed. Then he was utterly still. "JAMIE! Breathe, Goddammit," I shrieked when I jumped on him, pumping his chest. My shoulder screamed in pain until I just couldn't press anymore. I collapsed on him, on my husband, my lover, my best friend.

He jerked awake, eyes blinking. I found the flashlight, still glowing in the snow. Shining it at his face, I saw fresh blood burble out of the wound. "Get that light out of my eyes, will ya?"

His arm struck my hand, hard.

The flashlight flew out of my hand. I threw myself on him and he squeezed me back. "It's okay, hun, it's okay," he murmured. "Now find that torch and get up."

Torch? I'd never heard him use that term. It was lying half buried a foot away from us, but glowed faintly under the snow. I'd lost my glove when I was giving Jamie CPR. My hands were freezing and my shoulder throbbed.

"Come on, we better hurry. Grab my hand."

His hand was colder than mine. Icy. Sticky with blood. We trudged on.

As we stomped through the snow, I tried to calculate how far we'd gone, how far behind us the car was. I knew this terrain, the distance between roads. But in the snow we may be winding ourselves in zigzags and circles without knowing it. The light sometimes shone brightly ahead of us, sometimes dimly flickered. Was it even the same light? Was it really even there?

Numbness took me and I didn't shiver anymore. We didn't speak. I still held the light, fearing Jamie might have another seizure. I walked in front first, breaking path. Then he took a turn stomping. It was hard, cold going and then, finally, we were there.

We stood in a bright blue-lit patch of brilliant snow next to a two-story log cabin. But the yard light seemed to be the only light on. Struggling through unbroken snow to the front porch, we collapsed. I crawled to the front door and pounded with the flashlight. "Help, please help us."

No answer. Jamie seemed to have passed out again. I screamed and pounded. Nothing. The thought went through my brain even as I broke the window *if this was my home and someone hurt and cold was locked outside, I would hope they would break in.* A gush of warm air greeted me, making me shiver again. I climbed in, falling onto a hard wooden floor. I crawled to the front door and unlatched it, leaving it open as I dragged Jamie's heavy body through. I leaned him against the wall, closed the door and checked to see if there was electricity. Holding my breath, I flicked the switch. Nothing.

I tried a lamp. Nothing. The yard light was on a different system, as it was with most of these old cabins. The owners must have left for the winter and turned off the main power. It was okay, I told myself. First, tend to Jamie, then start a fire.

As if he read my mind, Jamie said, "I got the fire. Try to find a phone." A welcoming blaze lit up the room. I watched for a second while Jamie wrestled log after log onto the fire. The light grew brighter. It illuminated his face, the ghostly pale contrasting starkly against the blackened blood around the horrible wound. I wondered if he would lose any function.

In the new light I found an old table phone on the kitchen counter. I picked up the receiver. No dial tone. Some of these lines had a soft dial when disconnected that reach emergency services. I punched in 911. No connection.

"Becca, come over here." Jamie motioned to me with a pale hand. "We'll cuddle. In the morning we'll get the help we need. Come on."

I went to him. He pulled several blankets and pillows from the couch onto the floor in front of the fireplace. Throwing one over himself he put his arm around me and pulled me closer to him. We sat down and pulled more blankets around us. He was still cold, colder than I was, so I snuggled up more closely. It wasn't until that moment I realized how tired and sore I was. My head rested on his chest; his arms encircled me.

"Jamie, will you be okay if I sleep? I'm just so tired."

"Sleep, dear. I'm fine. And Rebecca, you will be fine, too. Never forget that."

*****

Glaring light seared into my head when I opened my eyes. Pain shot through my shoulder. I was trapped. Struggling, I heard a man's voice, "Rebecca? Rebecca Sinclair? Don't try to move. I'm Dennis Schroeder, EMT. You've been in an accident."

I settled back down, aware now of white sheets and a gurney under me. My neck was trapped in a brace, an IV flowed into my arm. "What's the damage?" I asked, looking around as much as I could. I saw another man taking my blood pressure and pulse.

"You have a fractured left clavicle, minor cuts to your face and hands. Your right hand suffered minor frost bite. There may be some closed brain trauma, but we won't know that until we run a full diagnostic."

Dennis moved aside and a large face replaced his. "Rebecca, I'm Captain Armistead, State Patrol. How did you get here? You're over three miles from where your car slid off the road."

I closed my eyes. "Captain, Jamie, my husband, he's…he didn't make it, did he?" I willed myself to look at him.

"No, Rebecca, he died in the crash. It was instantaneous. He never felt a thing."

Dennis' hand on my right shoulder held me down. "Shhh, now. Hold still. You are in good hands."

"But Jamie…he and I walked here from the car before the snow…we followed the yard light."

Dennis and the Captain looked over me at each other, exchanging a look I couldn't discern. The Captain said, "There is no yard light here. You walked alone miles to this abandoned cabin. There's no electricity."

I couldn't understand why these guys were telling me this. Jamie, his wound, his seizure, the phone. "I called 911 from the phone."

"There's no phone. You are a lucky, lucky young lady. The snow plow driver saw the roof of the car and called us. We followed your footprints through the snow. That's how we found you. Rest now. We're loading you into the ambulance. Your parents will meet us at the hospital."

SMALL ENDS

E. Cluff Elliott

Chapter 1

S imon Decker leaned against the steering wheel. Light from the dash illuminated his face in a blue-green glow. "You sure you want to do this?" His face wrinkled as he looked at the sheets of water dousing the windshield. Younger than his appearance, he had a brown crew cut peppered with gray and an overgrown mustache. The youthful glint in his eyes suggested there was plenty of life under his weathered skin. Despite years of bucking bales, horse-shoeing, and other manual labor jobs, his smile remained affable. He was one of those cowboys who made Wyoming proud.

Sitting at the opposite end of the Ford's bench seat Hattie, Simon's daughter, studied an open text book between disgusted looks at the rain. She was twelve, and Simon remembered a time when she lived for sheep riding and barrel racing, but because of her accelerated

143

learning ability, she was surrounded by kids two and three years older. The crowd explained her choice of black jeans, heavy metal t-shirts, and gothic jewelry—evidence that her rebelliousness had started as prematurely as her intelligence. Tonight she dressed in baggie jeans and a Black Sabbath t-shirt. Even though she listened to lyrically incomprehensible bands like Cannibal Corpse or Impending Doom, he would always see her as his little cowgirl, bright-eyed and determined. Simon was glad she wasn't into black makeup yet.

"You don't get it," she said, her disgust souring to anger. "If we don't get an owl pellet tonight, I'm not going to have a project to turn in."

Her science fair project was due Monday. She wanted to replicate the entire human circulatory system, complete with circulating pig's blood. But since she waited so long to get the project going, she decided to fall back on dissecting regurgitated owl pellets.

"Can the outburst, missy. That drama you pull on your mom ain't gonna work on me; you should know better than that. I am curious, though, how long ago did your teacher assign this project?" Simon turned off the truck and left the keys hanging in the ignition. At eight o'clock on a Sunday night in the mountains northwest of Wheatland, thieves were more likely to be attacked by a bear than steal anything.

"Two months," Hattie said avoiding eye contact—her normal reaction when she knew she'd been caught procrastinating on an important project.

Simon unbuckled and positioned his back against the door, bringing his right leg up so it rested part way across the seat. "So, because you waited until the last minute, you expect me to get out in this downpour? You better think again. I didn't bring you out here just so you can dump your scholastic pressures on your ol' man. You're the one that waited until the last minute."

For the first time since hopping into her father's Ford and making the forty-five minute journey Hattie lost some of her venom.

"Sorry, Dad." She sat back and sighed.

What people most often forgot about Hattie was her age. She might have the Periodic Table memorized, along with their respective atomic numbers, but that didn't mean she was expected to bypass adolescence.

"Don't be sorry. Regret is a powerful thing. It can teach, but it can also scare you into doing nothin', and then you're only hurtin' yourself. So, never be sorry for who you are. But, that also means you should own up to your actions."

"Even if you get in trouble?" Hattie asked, her face a playground of innocence.

"Especially, if it means trouble."

"I guess that means you know what happened in chemistry class, huh?"

"The call from Principal Dempsey kinda gave it away." Simon folded his arms across his chest. "What made you think to set your teacher's money on fire, anyway?"

Hattie smirked. "It wasn't supposed to happen that way. I read online that you can soak a dollar bill in a mixture of rubbing alcohol and water and set it on fire without damaging the bill, but the mixture wasn't quite right."

Simon felt a knot in his brain try to untie itself as he pictured his daughter at the front of the class with a grin on her face. "You didn't explain to your teacher what you were doing?"

"Yeah, but I didn't know he was going to hand me a fifty dollar bill."

"A fifty?" said Simon. "And you didn't think about asking him for something smaller?"

"It's his fault."

"Were the burnt floor tiles his fault too? Or was that just part of your mixture mishap?"

"I thought they looked better toasted," she half-mumbled.

"Excuses and sarcasm aren't helping you right now. You had no right to do what you did. You're a smart girl, Hattie. You know you're a smart girl. But you don't own a license allowing you to experiment your every whim."

She looked defeated. Her face drooped and her bottom jaw pushed forward. "So what's going to happen?"

"Well, I'm not the one you should be concerned about."

Her face jerked up, eyes wide and worried. "Does Mom know yet?"

"No, I don't reckon she does, but her ignorance ain't gonna last. I'm sure the school's sending a letter to the house."

Hattie's preteen emotions erupted. "What do I do? You know she's going to flip."

"Well, I reckon we'll sit here and talk about what needs to be talked about. Then, if the weather clears…we'll see how I feel."

"Come on, Dad. What about the owl pellets? Dissecting one of these things is supposed to be as interesting as opening the belly of a whale or a shark or a crocodile." Her voice grew more excited with each animal, showing her level of maturity was still that of a twelve-year-old.

Simon wrinkled his face in revulsion. He'd gutted his fair share of wild game, but he didn't see any reason to cut open their stomach and see what they ate. "Let's stick with owl pellets. Now, you ready to do this?"

Hattie sighed. "Yeah, let's get this over with."

"No, this isn't a *let's get this over with* moment; those moments are reserved for chores and homework. This is a *if you can't listen to what dad says he may go back to corporal punishment* moment. I'm giving you a chance, Hattie. Your mother and I just want what's best for you."

Chapter 2

The two of them talked for close to an hour, first about how Hattie planned on paying back her teacher, and second about the extra chores in her future. After that Simon reminisced about the glory days when he'd tried his luck on the back of a bucking bronco. Hattie listened with hypnotized admiration. After a brief pause in conversation they noticed the silence. The rain had stopped.

With a grin bright enough to outshine the Ford's headlights, Hattie turned to her father and clapped her hands together in supplication. "Pleeeeease, can we go look for owl pellets now? We've been talking for a really long time."

Simon pretended to think about it for a minute, gazing out his window studying the surrounding area. "I don't know, it's gettin' *real* late."

"Come on, Dad, it won't take long. Let's just find two or three and then we can go."

He faked a yawn and stretched his arms. "Maybe we should ask around the neighborhood. See if they have any pellets."

She didn't answer, just folded her arms across her chest and scowled.

"Fine, let's go," said Simon making a show of his decision. He relished moments like this, watching joy spread across his daughter's face.

"Yes. You're the best, Dad!" Hattie pulled her backpack up from the floorboard and started digging out supplies.

After putting on rubber gloves and stuffing sealable baggies in their pockets, they grabbed identical black flashlights and piled out of the truck.

Covered with wild buffalo grass, the clearing was dotted with a variety of plant life. Fire-red flowers on Indian Paintbrush glinted with moisture as beams of light played off their surfaces. Buckbrush, its small branches covered in clusters of tiny white blooms, looked like a giant snowball left over from winter. As they made their way across the clearing—their pants soaking up water like sponges—they saw Kinnikinnick bushes blanketing exposed bedrock. The bushes were bare of fruit, which meant wildlife frequented the area, possibly dangerous wildlife, but without tracks or some other proof, there was no way to tell what lived nearby.

Ten feet beyond the tree line Simon noted Quaking Aspen among the pines. The aspens were dying out as the Ponderosas grew back—effects of a forest fire nearly four decades earlier.

"Don't go too far." He watched Hattie's outline bounce away to the right. If not for the flashlight she carried, he wasn't sure he'd see her at all.

"If I see Bigfoot, I promise I'll run back to the truck as fast as I can." She paused at the base of a pine, used her light to examine the ground, and then dash toward the next tree.

Copying his daughter's actions, he continued to the left, using his boots to brush aside foliage. He wasn't sure they'd find anything, but three trees later he spotted a pellet. It looked like an oversized hairball with bits of bone poking through fur. He picked it up and pinched it between his gloved fingers. The disturbance released a stench of vomit that made him gag. Rushing to open the plastic baggie and store the sour reek, he turned his head and gasped for fresh air.

"Oh my God! Dad! You got to come see this."

Simon was all too happy to flee the stink persisting around him. He followed the beam of her light and excited giggles. Then she was there, a dark shadow illuminated by light, pointing to what had to be the world's largest owl pellet, a regurgitated sphere of undigested bone and fur the size of a softball.

"That can't be real." He crouched down to inspect it.

"Only one way to find out," Hattie suggested, grinning.

Simon squeezed the pellet. It felt like the smaller one he'd found, and just as rain soaked, but where did it come from? It didn't smell the same. The reek of vomit was faint. And then there was the size to consider. If the small pellet came from an owl between twenty and twenty-five inches tall, how big was the bird that made a pellet five times that size?

Hattie sensed his reluctance because her grin suddenly changed to a frown. "Come on, Dad. Don't tell me you're scared. Everything in there is already dead, remember?"

"My ma always told me to leave the dead alone."

"You *are* scared." She grinned again.

"Dads don't get scared," said Simon, more to bolster his courage than confirm his daughter's speculations. She was right. He was being a chicken.

"Does that mean we can take it?"

"Bag it up," he said. "But do your old man a favor, okay? Don't tell your Mom I got the heebie-jeebies. I'd never hear the end of it."

Chapter 3

Hattie opened the passenger door on the truck and tossed the baggies onto the floor. Dome lights spilled out making harsh lines on the ground. Her black attire was completely visible again, but that wasn't the only thing revealed. Radiant with confidence, Hattie Decker wore a smirk of morbid curiosity.

"What do you think we're gonna find in the big pellet?"

"Who knows, kiddo?" Simon opened his door and stashed the flashlights, secretly admiring the joy on his daughter's face. To him it was a sign that life was good and he was doing his job as a father. And as a father, he decided, nothing could be better. He noticed her watching him with inquisitive eyes, as if he should add something insightful. "Well, we're not dissecting it up here in the mountains. You're just gonna have to get them home, aren't you?"

Hattie's grin was wider than ever. "You got that right." She hopped inside and closed the door behind her. "What if we find a finger bone?"

"What?"

"You know, like if the owl found a shallow grave or a murder site. It swoops in smelling blood." She hooked her thumbs together and flapped her fingers like wings; the jewelry on her wrists jingled like small bells. "It pokes around making sure its prey is dead. Then, with a quick snap it breaks off the ring finger and swallows it whole."

"Um, let's stick with small critters," he said. The details his daughter could come up with might be gruesome, but the creativity she used never failed to impress him.

"Yeah," she admitted, ducking her head a little, "I'm not sure if I could handle a human finger, but it'd be a cool story to tell everyone at school."

Simon imagined three jointed bones lodged in the giant pellet. He pictured a wedding ring with an inscription engraved on the inside curve. As the dome light flipped off, he realized he was holding his breath.

"You doing okay?" she asked.

"Yep, I think both of us have been awake far too long. Let's go home," he said breathing again. The huge owl pellet might be unusually large, and it may or may not contain a human finger, but he was done feeling spooked out here.

Simon's heart skipped a beat as something large and heavy caved in the hood with a metallic thud. Contents rattled as the truck rocked under the impact. Hattie screamed with the terrified pitch found in nightmares and horror movies.

Outside, the creature turned and fluttered an expanse of wings wider than the truck. Recognizable only by its shape, shadows covered the bulk of its body. It was a bird of some kind, but the sounds it created were unlike anything they'd heard from other birds. Enormous wings flapped like a flag whipping in a heavy gust. Metal screeched as talons cut gouges into the hood. With an eerie motion, it swiveled its head ninety degrees to the right, and looked at them, yellow eyes glowing like phosphorescent orbs.

Hattie hugged her knees to her chest and yelled. She repeated the same two words over and over again, turning an exclamatory sentence into a continuous stream of panicked dialogue. "GoDadGoDadGoDadGoDadGoDad!"

The bird swung its head from side-to-side in a figure eight pattern, its weight rocking the truck.

Reaching for the ignition, Simon jammed his index and ring fingers against the steering column. His screamed as pain traveled all the way to his elbow, immobilizing his forearm in waves of numbness.

"WHAT.... What's wrong?"

Simon ignored her and used his left hand to find the ignition. Feeling the keys dangling from the column like a tongue, he seized them and turned the switch.

The truck responded, rumbled, tried to idle, then died with a shudder.

"Daaad!"

Simon looked up at a giant owl on the other side of the windshield. Above the owl's hooked beak, its eyes were orbs of coal surrounded by the lusty yellow of gold. Each looming eyeball looked as big as Simon's fist. The damned thing had snuck up on them, ambushed them.

He tried the key again; the engine groaned and turned.

Reacting to the truck beneath it, the feathers around the bird's neck flared out to the size of a basketball. Most disturbing was the way the copper feathers around its eyes seemed to rotate toward each other like cogs in a machine.

"Come on. Come on," he said as he pumped the gas pedal, hoping he wasn't flooding the engine. Even as he tried again to get the engine to turn over, the impulse to watch those eyes mesmerized him. The rotating illusion grew hypnotic.

Beside him, Hattie's grip on her knees loosened as her body swayed. "Wow, check out its eyes, Dad. They look so cool." Her voice was slow and deliberate. Her panic gone, replaced with a strange drowsiness like the effects of a strong sedative.

"Hattie, we need to snap out of it." He grabbed her shoulder and tried shaking her out of her stupor. Her head flopped as she moaned but that was it. "Hattie, come on, sweetie. Don't do this to me." The urge to look at the bird's eyes intensified. He wanted to see those perfect gears spinning in on each other like two galaxies on the edge of destruction. He wanted to see the dark centers of those galaxies. He wanted to fall into their lingering draw. Once his peripheral vision caught sight of the bird's performance all defenses dropped and his head turned to watch.

Outside, the bird moved with grace and agility, stretching its wings until they covered the windshield. Its feathers created a design of alternating browns and tans. Each shade was distinct from those around it, the edges clearly separating one color from the next.

Next to him, Hattie lost consciousness and slumped against the door. His instinct as a father demanded something be done, but his willpower against the owl faded with its vibrating wings. The clear and distinct lines separating brown and tan feathers blended together until the pixilated colors morphed into an uneven blur of static.

The epileptic bursts and shifting patterns pulled at Simon and locked his eyes into a stare that couldn't be broken—heavy and relentless. He was sore and tired. Legs that functioned well enough to pump the gas pedal grew numb. Determined hands fell limp. His body, once tensed to the point of snapping, grew slack. Despite the growing fatigue, he began to understand the connection between the owl's aggressive dance and the hypnosis he and his daughter felt.

All too aware of the silence, he reached for Hattie but his shaky right hand only made it as far as the seat between them. It was like having a hundred pound weight attached to his wrist. "Why are you doing this to us?"

The bird rose to its full height and pulled its shoulders back, wings still vibrating. The high-pitched shrieking that came from its open beak was similar to the creak of a rusty metal door the size of a house.

Half grunting, half yelling, Simon gathered his strength and moved his hand to the steering column. He grabbed the keys in the ignition, but he could barely feel the thin metal between his fingertips. Everything was numb.

"Come on you stupid keys, turn." The Ford roared to life, as if challenging Simon's insult.

The bird shrieked its frustration as the engine revved twice burning off gas. It fluttered and danced, trying to assert its strange hypnotic control.

Simon felt the trance begin to clear away. Clouds that blocked rational thinking were lifting like fog in a pervasive wind. This was their chance to escape.

Simon put the truck in reverse and stomped on the gas pedal.

The bird grappled across the hood, its talons searching for purchase. Unable to find balance, it cupped the air with its wings, took flight and disappeared.

Caught between finding safety and making sure his daughter was okay, Simon hit the brakes and flipped on the dome light.

"Hattie?" He leaned over and shook her, watchful of the owl's return. "Wake up. Hattie!"

She sat up and rubbed her eyes with the heels of her hands. "Dad? What happened to the bird?"

Chapter 4

On the ride home, Hattie seemed out of character. When she was four she owned a Gizmo doll—the popular creature called a Mogwai from the equally popular movie *Gremlins*. After days of pleading from cute little Hattie in her pigtails and tiny cowboy boots, Simon made the mistake of letting her watch the first *Gremlins* movie. It gave her nightmares for weeks. Now, in wake of surviving an attack from the largest predator in the night skies she remained calm, collected, she hummed to herself. She didn't seem scared, so what was it, disbelief or denial? Simon didn't think it was that either, but he also didn't have anything else to go on.

"You ever heard of an owl that big?" Simon asked. He wanted recognition that the attack happened, that he wasn't crazy and imagined the whole thing.

"I don't think we need to worry about it." She never tried to make eye contact; she just faced the road ahead with a strange sort of grin. "It'd probably be easier to just forget about it. I mean, who's going to believe a story about an owl that stands as tall as me. Would you believe a story like that before tonight?" Pulling her arms part way into the air, she began to dance in place to some song only she could hear. "Just do what I'm doing and forget about the owl. Come on, Dad."

Simon played along with Hattie but he couldn't forget what had happened. He kept playing it over in his head, trying to make sense of it. He asked himself what would've happened if both of them had fallen asleep out there. What would've happened if that thing got into the cab? Would they be dead? As easily as the bird's talons scratched through the hood of the truck, he expected so. But why, what was it after? He didn't know, couldn't even begin to know. He suspected it might have something to do with the giant pellet they found in the mountains.

Once they got back to Wheatland, Simon parked the truck in front of their white stucco ranch house. Dim light from street posts cast erratic shadows and familiar silhouettes across red shingles and manicured grass. Toys and bikes created an obstacle course. With four kids living in the house, it was amazing the grass could be seen at all.

Hattie raced ahead, hopping over toys to get to the door. She paused long enough to kick a bouncy ball toward the line of fruit trees along the northern edge of the property.

Simon got out and inspected the hood before following his daughter. The gouges in the metal were narrow, maybe an inch wide at their widest point. Up in the mountains it sounded like the hood should be in shreds but it wasn't. All the commotion resulted in a total of two official gouges, each of them less than six inches long. The scratches and indentations beat that number by about twenty. It was more than he wanted to deal with at the moment.

"Come on, Dad. I want to cut this bad boy open." Hattie held up the baggie holding the largest pellet. The round, hair-covered bulb looked alien behind plastic, like it was in the midst of evolution.

"I'm comin'," Simon answered.

Holding the screen door open, Hattie started bouncing in place, keeping herself contained as well as a Chihuahua on a high caffeine diet.

"Having problems?" Simon teased as he unlocked the front door.

Hattie darted into the living room and dropped the baggies on the beige sofa.

"Hey, no, that's not where those go," said Simon. "What the devil would your mom say, if she saw you put those nasty things on her couch?"

Hattie picked up the baggies but ignored his question. Swinging the pellets she looked around the living room as though she were missing something. "Where is everyone?"

"At GiGi's," he said, shutting the door and putting his keys in his pocket. When he turned back, Hattie wore a confused expression.

"When I told your mom what we planned on doing tonight she nearly lost her beans. Once she stopped gagging, she said she was gonna take the other kids to GiGi's for the night. Your mother never had the stomach I have." *It was just as well after the weirdness with the bird.* He wanted some time to make sense of everything, not to mention think of a good explanation for the damaged hood.

"I wish I could've seen mom's face." Still swinging the baggies, Hattie headed into the kitchen, talking as she went. "I love watching her get all grossed out over this kind of stuff. What about Tara and Lisa and Jon?"

This time the memory made Simon laugh. To date, he'd never seen Tara so pale. He didn't have to tell Hattie that, however. No sense in over-feeding her ego.

"What's so funny?" There was suspicion in her voice.

"Let's just say, none of them share your curiosity."

Chapter 5

Simon found a can of lemon scented disinfectant and set it on the table with the dissecting tools. The last thing he wanted to do was to throw up all over his daughter's project. No one deserved to have to suffer through the smell of owl *and* human vomit at the same time.

Hattie sat at the table facing away from the back door. Jewelry replaced with surgical gloves, she measured the pellets through the baggies using a pink ruler. The one Simon found was close to three inches long and shaped like a dog turd. Hattie's whopper of a pellet measured a full six and a half inches.

The difference between the two sizes worried Simon, but what was he supposed to do? He could focus on the strangeness of the situation and drive himself crazy, or he could do what his daughter was doing and try to move on. He thought about the monstrous bird out there somewhere. Could it cough up a pellet that big?

Hattie used a set of BBQ tongs to extract the pellets from the baggies and set them on paper plates. She would've torn straight into the giant pellet had Simon not stopped her.

"Let's practice on the small one first." He wanted to take the huge lump of regurgitated hair and bone and shove it down the garbage disposal. The more he thought about the thing the more he wanted to get rid of it, but he restrained himself. If his daughter could endure the experience, then so could he.

Hattie agreed. She pulled the paper plate with the small pellet over, grabbed the lemon spray, and started to apply a tide of cleanliness. In the bright light of the kitchen it was easier to make out more detail on the small pellet which actually turned out to hold some pretty cool information. They found a group of spines and rib cages the size of a large thumbnail, perhaps the remnants of a nest of rodents, mice.

Simon pictured an owl as it discovered the nest and proceeded to gobble down the tiny pink treats whole. It made him wonder how much meat the huge owl in the mountains could swallow whole.

"Finally," Hattie said as she switched plates. "Let's see what this bad boy's got. I bet all the interesting stuff is in this one."

Feeling something like apprehension mixed with fear and doubt, Simon helped his daughter as they cut into the spongy pellet. He used an X-Acto knife to cut through hair and fur while Hattie poked around for bones using her mother's Mary Kay tweezers. Fibers ripped like Velcro. They sprayed disinfectant until the scent of lemons filled the kitchen. After an hour, they had several piles of tiny bones, a mound of beetle exoskeletons, a small mountain of hair and fur, and one skull. If it were a mouse or squirrel, the skull would have large incisors and a pointed bone structure. The teeth on this skull were flat and followed the curve of its jaw. The nose area was a triangular hole. And the cranial bone structure was round, almost like a miniature bowling ball.

They stared at the small skull and then at each other.

"It's got to be some kind of snub-nosed field rat," Hattie said sitting back in her seat and shaking her head in disbelief. She kept folding and unfolding her arms as if she wasn't sure what to do with them.

Simon, with thirty years on his daughter and a bit more practicality, began sorting out bones. He didn't have a perfect recollection of his old high school anatomy classes but he remembered enough to get a rough idea.

Hattie sat forward, elbows on the table as she looked on with interest. "What are you doing?"

Simon didn't answer. Tunnel vision gripped him in a whirlpool of skepticism. The kitchen table seemed as large as a football field. Sound dimmed to a dull drone, except for his shallow breathing. One bone after another, everything fell into place. Tibias and femurs, and ribs, but it didn't stop there. Simon had Hattie hold an old magnifying glass up so he could use tweezers to line up tiny spinal segments, fitting them to a pelvic girdle that was perhaps a couple inches wide. Bone by bone, he worked until more than half the pile was gone, revealing a nine-inch humanoid skeleton.

There it was. The impossible thing before him justified his fears, and was a free ticket to insanity. His mother's good advice repeated in his head, firm, and irrefutable: *Leave the dead alone, Simon. Unless you want to earn yourself an early grave, it's best to leave the dead alone.*

Hattie was saying something, but Simon didn't hear her.

"We need to get rid of this," he sat back shaking his head. The impossibility of their discovery rocked his understanding of the world in a way that made him more than uncomfortable. He felt positively terrified. "We can dump it in the sticks behind the house. I'll call your teacher and see if we can get you another week for your project. No one can know about this, not your mom, not your sisters or brother, no one."

"DAD," Hattie yelled. She was on the edge of hysteria.

Concentration broken, Simon looked to his daughter.

Hattie's face was serious, red in the cheeks, and pale around the edges. She'd been trying to get his attention for some time. Her animated arms pointed and waved about in desperation. Turning in his seat, he saw why.

Beyond the double French doors that led to the backyard, the bird that attacked them on the mountain stood on the porch watching them in wide-eyed silence. Patio light illuminated its body as if the 100 watt bulb suddenly became a small sun. Every inch was clear; every detail perfect. Distinct feathers hued in browns, greys, and whites layered its chest like scales. Black and copper ear tufts angled up like horns, creating a V shape above a hooked beak at least five inches long. Two ribbons of light reflected down the ebony slope of its beak.

"What is that thing doing all the way down here?" Simon whispered.

The giant Great-Horned Owl stood at their back door like a sentry. The presence of the bird up in the mountains had mesmerized them. Here in the light, the impossible size of the bird was intimidating enough to make Simon feel like a child again, when all perceptions suffer gigantism.

"Did it follow us?" Hattie's voice wavered with apprehension. She clenched the backrest on the chair, eyebrows so high on her

158

forehead Simon thought they might pop off. She looked like she was on a roller coaster, ready for the knuckle-white ride of her life.

Not bothering to answer, Simon glared at the beast. He press his lips into a thin line. His nostrils flared.

Leave the dead alone, Simon.

The owl winked at them, one fist-sized eye at a time.

He thought about calling Animal Control to come take their stalker away, but what was he going to say? *There's a giant owl in my backyard; can you please come get it?* He might get a response but it would probably be a police cruiser that pulled up to the house, and it would be to restrain him, not the owl, because owl's that size don't exist, can't exist.

"Foul creature." The voice was not Hattie's. It was lower in tone, almost a complete octave below her smooth alto.

Simon and Hattie spun in their seats, knees banging together. On the table in front of them, a bit taller than a Venti cup from Starbucks, a blue figure of a man grinned from underneath a wild tuft of hair. His body was ethereal as though his image were being projected on wisps of blue-gray smoke, gaining density and shape, thickening only to dissipate on some hidden current.

Simon stared at the smoke and rubbed his eyes. He couldn't believe what he was seeing. The appearance of the owl was bad enough. Now there was this apparition.

"You aren't deaf, are you?" The little blue man pushed himself up, floating in the air like a ghost. Long arms dropped to his side as thin legs unfolded beneath him. A skinny but muscular chest slouched over the top of a bloated belly. The image was disproportionate and eerie, unnatural.

Simon swiped at the blue man, his hand rushing through the air like a flyswatter. Fear of what the smoke might do to him made him pull back. The form swirled into nothingness for a moment, catching the air currents and dispersing before swimming back into a cloud.

"It won't do any good," the form said as if explaining to a child.

159

Simon swiped again with more confidence, determined to prove the thing wrong. Smoke puffed its way to the opposite side of the table. Once it reached the edge, it stopped then circulated back to its original location. Hattie's hand stopped him from swiping a third time, catching his forearm halfway through the swing.

"Don't." Letting go of her dad's arm, she pulled her gloves off with a snap and pointed to the table. "The bones are gone. Don't you get it? The bones you put together are gone. Look."

She was right. The skeleton Simon labored to assemble was gone.

"Kid catches on quick," the voice said as its form coalesced on the table. "But my bones are the least of your problems."

"I'm gonna show you problems." Simon reached back for another swipe at the blue smoke. *Bones that mutate into blue vapor have no right to exist. It wasn't possible yesterday, so why should today be any different?* Regardless, he meant to swat at it until it dissipated like smoke from a campfire.

Hattie stood up and threw herself in harm's way. "STOP IT! Dad! Stop. I think we better listen to him."

"This isn't real, Hattie. I don't know what we got into up there on the mountain, but whatever it is it's makin' us see things. We've been drugged. That's the only explanation. It has to be. It's—"

Hattie's bare hands cupped his cheeks. Her face came into view like the light of a freight train moving through the jet black tunnel of her hair. "I know what you're feeling, Dad, I really do, but I think he's right." Gently, she turned his head to follow the direction of her own gaze.

While they were focused on the smoke, they neglected to notice the activity at their back door. Alongside the huge owl that tried to hypnotize them, other normal-sized owls landed on the patio every few seconds. The assortment was wide, their differences many. All were silent.

160

"Like I said, your problems are bigger than missing bones." Regarding them with a nervous grin, the reestablished cloud backed toward a pile of fur.

The giant owl began pecking at the glass, its beak *ticking* with a creepy repetition that seemed to beg entry: *Please, sir. Let me in. I'll be good. I'll be a good owl. I'll pick up after myself. But Please, PLEASE LET ME IN!*

Crash.

One of the glass panes broke loose and shattered on the floor.

Simon jumped to his feet and scrambled away from the table. Dragging Hattie with him, he knocked aside both chairs in retreat.

Hattie screamed and dodged chair-legs.

The owl pecked with calculated jabs, *ticking* through glass panes as if they were paper. Shards fell and shattered, exciting the smaller owls until they flapped around in encouragement.

Simon flinched as another pane of glass crashed to the floor. "Why is it trying to come in?" He scowled at the little creature of smoke.

Wide-eyed under his tuft of hair, it jerked its head in a direction away from the owls. "Take me out of here and I'll tell you everything. It's that or we all die when they break through."

Simon heard genuine fear in the apparition's voice, but he failed to understand why. *Why would a ghost fear owls?*

Hattie pulled free and gained her footing. She looked at her father with defiance in her eyes.

"What are you doing?" Simon grabbed his daughter's shoulder and started hauling her toward the living room. "We have to get out of here. If that thing comes through and we're still in the kitchen, it's gonna tear us to pieces."

"We can't leave without *him*," Hattie said wrenching her shoulder free and running back to the table.

"Him who? It's a ghost, Hattie. There's no such thing as ghosts."

She turned, cupped her hands together, and lowered them to the table. The small collection of blue smoke gripped her thumb and climbed aboard.

Wood cracked as the owl used its talons to grip the mullions, ripping them from the door's frame. Soon there would be a hole big enough to fit through.

"Fine, let's go," Simon said gritting his teeth.

Hattie started out of the dining area and into the living room, carrying the column of blue smoke in her hands.

Simon reached the hall and then stopped when the big owl screeched in triumph. He turned to see the owl swivel its head from side to side before leaping onto the table and pecking at the dissected pellets. Wings flapping, it shrieked and began to look curiously around the room. Fur, beetle shells, and tiny bones scattered across the table as the downdraft from the owl's wings made a mess of the kitchen. Notes on the fridge rustled, pictures on the walls rattled. The owl's yellow eyes centered on Simon.

"Out front, Hattie! Go for the truck!"

He backed away from the owl as it lowered its stance and tucked its wings behind its body. Its feathers vibrated like the tail of a rattlesnake.

Simon ran.

Moving through the front door, he tried reaching in his pocket for the keys but the rubber gloves kept gripping fabric, refusing to let his hand enter.

He paused partway across the lawn and pulled at the gloves. The rubber snapped against his wrist twice before peeling off. He tossed them to the side. Hands searched with frantic slaps and pats at his thighs and butt. Fear in the pit of his stomach grew when he failed to find the keys. "Come on, where are they?"

Ahead of him, Hattie reached the Ford and climbed inside.

Behind him, the enormous owl tore through the house. Sounds of destruction accompanied its shrieks of rage. Between the loud thuds and crashes there was a chorus of smaller wings punctuated by the occasional squawk.

He looked back to see the first of the little owls fly over the house in a tall swoop. The figure adjusted its course, targeted him, then picked up speed shooting through open space like a missile.

Forgetting about the keys he sprinted for the truck, heart pumping, arms flailing over his head for protection. One, two, three talons raked his head as he zigzagged toward the street. Touching the wounds under his hair, he circled the truck and climbed in, slamming the door shut. The cuts were shallow and short, yet when his condition became apparent to his daughter, she reacted as if his head had been split.

"OH MY GOD, DAD." She leaned over, wiped blood from his temple onto her black jeans. "Are you okay?"

"Don't worry about the small ones," the blue apparition said sitting between them at the top of the bench seat with its back against the window.

A creepy barn owl—the kind Hollywood likes to use in alien movies—landed on the hood next to the gouges its leader had made earlier and looked at them.

Hattie squealed and jumped back in her seat.

"Not that one either," said the apparition. "Though, it's probably the one that scratched your head."

Simon slapped at his pockets again, ignoring the little wretch. "Shoulda left the dead alone," he mumbled under his breath. "Ma always told me, but did I listen? No!" The keys were there, he felt the familiar bulge in his left pocket. Sudden adrenalin pulsed through his body as he reached in and yanked the key ring free. "YES," he yelled as he found the ignition key and shoved it into the steering column.

The truck responded with a familiar shudder as two more owls landed on the hood. The three owls stared at them with unreadable gold eyes.

On the edge of tears, Hattie pulled her knees up and tucked her head down.

"No, they're not important either," said the smoke.

"Come on you stupid damn truck, START." Simon felt a rush of emotions: desperation, fear, excitement. He remembered how the truck had acted up on the mountain, he remembered how long it took to start, he remembered what could happen if their damned leader caught up to them. "START. START."

Engine rumbling to life, Simon hit the gas pedal and forced the gearshift into drive. Lurching, the truck squealed its tires, bounced against the curb, and found traction. The truck accelerated and all four owls took flight. When he looked back, the giant owl came crashing through the screen door, ripping it from its hinges and getting tangled in its splintered remains.

"You could've closed the front door behind you," said the blue smoke still sitting with his shoulders against the back window.

"Shut up, pipsqueak." Simon said. "I don't need advice from somethin' that hatched five minutes ago. Don't you think I see the damned thing?"

The owl tried to free itself, flapping wildly, but the screen refused to let go.

"The name's Tel-ba, not pipsqueak."

Chapter 6

Less than a mile down the road, the silence in the truck was heavy as a lead cocoon, tight and uncomfortable. Hattie contributed by staring out the window at the wheatgrass and sagebrush, her back angled toward her father. The blue smoke named Tel-ba did his part by keeping his nose pointed out the back window.

Simon tried to keep his head on straight, but he felt like he was in the *Twilight Zone*. He wanted his old life back. He wanted a ranch with no broken bones, easy births for livestock, soft soil to plant fence posts, and a Wyoming sunset from horseback. He wanted sanity.

On the edge of town, Simon turned into the Comfort Inn. The lot was half empty, lifeless. Strong halogen lights covered every inch of the pavement, spreading out into the night beyond.

Hattie surveyed the parking lot, surprise on her young face. "What are we doing?"

Finding a parking spot across from the building, Simon put the truck in park and turned to his daughter. "I'm not driving another yard until I start getting answers." He straightened his back against the seat and folded his arms, jaw clenching and unclenching. Weathered crow's feet appeared at the corners of his eyes as he waited.

"Don't look at me. I'm not the one who put the stupid skeleton together," she said.

"I think she's pointing the finger at you, old man," said Tel-ba.

"You better start explaining, pipsqueak. Either that, or I roll the windows down and turn the AC on high. What do you think? Should we watch you float out of here like a leaf in the wind?" Simon leaned for the dash. He wasn't sure if the little ghost could be blown away, but he had no problem trying.

"Alright, alright, nosy humans, what do you want to know?" Tel-ba held his long arms up in defense and grinned. "Do you want to know how you're going to die if you don't defend me? How the owls will pick your bones clean if you do not aid me? How you will..."

Simon rolled down the windows letting in a light breeze. The collection of blue smoke grew a tail as it caught the current. Tel-ba cringed and huddled against the seat attempting to hold on to something. Simon stopped. "Let's start with you, partner. What the hell are you? After we get that one cleared I might just roll up the window. What do you say? Are you gonna swirl on the bench or blow in the breeze?"

"Don't think because you're bigger, you're also smarter." Tel-ba scowled as if he'd tasted something rotten. "My race was alive and flourishing when Man lived in caves and grunted to each other."

Simon rolled the windows down a couple more inches.

"He's a Cambion," Hattie blurted, covering her mouth with both hands. Her eyes darted downward as if unsure from where the words were coming. She looked confused.

Simon eyed his daughter. "What's a Cambion?"

The expression on Hattie's face turned from confusion to bafflement to concentration. "I don't...I don't know."

"I do," said Tel-ba. He assembled into a sitting position, his torso fading then vanishing all together, making him look as though his two halves were connected by an imaginary umbilicus.

"Yeah, but why does my daughter know?" Simon reached for the AC switch.

"She is the one who found my pellet; therefore, she is the one who knows about us." Tel-ba sounded mad, his voice rising to a commanding tone that threatened Simon's alpha status. "If you had found the pellet, you would be the one who knows about us. That's just the way it works. When someone of my race dies, we have to have a guide to achieve resurrection."

"Well, undo it then. Pick someone else," Simon demanded.

"Cambion are an ancient people," said Tel-ba as his torso thickened back into existence. "And as an ancient race we are ruled by different laws. What is done cannot be undone."

"That's not acceptable you little runt," said Simon looming over the blue smoke.

"It doesn't matter if it's acceptable, old man. It's happening."

Simon knew Tel-ba was right. For the first time, he didn't feel like the adult. Love for his daughter was still there, mixed with confusion, and about a dozen other emotions, but he didn't know how to handle this situation. He felt lost in a world suddenly full of impossibilities.

"Think of this as only a side effect of the connection between your daughter and me. It's a knowing, harmless. Think of it as orientation when you start a new job. It's the hands-free introduction system to educate new members. It'll familiarize her with our kind, that's all."

"You little son of a bitch."

"Dad!" Hattie used the reprimanding tone she reserved to underline her deepest desires, a tone that threatened scorn if he didn't cool his temper. "It's okay. You can trust him. It's the owls we need to worry about."

"How do you know that?" Simon stared into his daughter's eyes. There was a powerful change happening behind those eyes. The sight ignited his emotions, a fire on the edge of flaring out of control. For her sake he reined in an urge to hogtie her and find her mother.

"I know because he showed me," Hattie said, her first tear streaming down her cheek. "Hundreds of them end up in owl pellets. And every year their numbers get smaller. *From out of the night, riding the silent air, the owls come and bring death with them.*"

"Why do they hunt you? Do you take their kids the same way you're trying to take mine?" Simon directed the question to Tel-ba but kept an eye on his daughter. This time he knew the words coming from his daughter's lips were not hers; she sounded distant as if being spoon fed words through an invisible earpiece.

"Because they think we're evil." Tel-ba dipped his head down as if the admission shamed him. "The ones who attacked you are a perfect example of what I'm talking about. Since the dawn of man, we've been on the run. Now, we're only a handful of vagrant tribes scattered across the globe. We're far from being a threat, but still the owls hunt us."

"Stupid birds." Hattie sniffled and wiped at the corners of her eyes.

"But what's it got to do with us?" Before the Cambion could answer, Simon turned to Hattie and added, "That means you need to keep quiet, got it?"

Hattie hesitated, glanced around the parking lot—wet eyes gleaming—then turned back to Simon and nodded.

Switching his attention to Tel-ba, Simon added, "Now talk."

"Ten-thousand years ago, at the turn of my people's Great War, our capital city at the Peak of Black Mountain faced an enormous threat.

Owls cut off our supplies. Losing the war could not be avoided. Instead of retaliation we focused on dispersal and preservation. Risking exposure to daylight, a time least likely to encounter our enemy, the tribe sent out small groups to build new homes. Over time, our once formidable group of Cambion dwindled. To survive, our homes were abandoned. We fled the city, but not the mountain. Lost and starving, every passing breath tasted of extinction. With so few, our defeat was inevitable. That's when the sanctuary was found and the prophecy was made." The blue smoke wrinkled his sloped forehead and gazed upward as if in supplication.

"We just hatched you out of a regurgitated hairball," Simon pointed out. "You make it sound as if you were there."

"I was there," said Tel-ba. "Ten-thousand years ago, on a mountain peak near where you found me, I was there to hear the prophecy; I was there to hear the words:

> *Forever to wander the green forest garden;*
> *our Resurrection's guided, our future's uncertain.*
> *Cambions shall endure to find their Zion,*
> *yet trials and hardships lay on the horizon.*
> *After futile attempts for thousands of years;*
> *after tasting nothing but our most bitter fears,*
> *we'll find a girl whose soul is true, and*
> *bring an end to Cambion solitude.*

Your daughter is the soul we've been looking for."

"This is ridiculous." Exasperated, Simon threw his hands up and looked out the front window. Turning back to Hattie, anger rising, he added, "If your mother was—"

A hand, fat as a club, knocked on the half-open window next to Simon. Hattie yelped, throwing herself backward and covering her face as if there were a ball zooming in her direction. Simon jumped, banging his knees against the steering wheel, adding to the pain he already felt at the top of his head. The commotion created enough air currents to blow Tel-ba away. His little blue collection of smoke dissipated then disappeared.

"You've got to be kidding me." Simon turned in his seat to find the owner of the hand taking a step back from the truck. The oval face, as chubby as the knocking fist, called forth images of Alfred Hitchcock, though not as old. Folds of fat and skin jiggled under his chin like udders full of milk. His eyes were just as bovine as his double chin: wide, glossy and unreadable. What his eyes didn't say, however, the badge that read Security on his breast pocket did. It sparkled with light from a parking lot halogen reflecting off its surface. This was a man that took his job seriously, wearing a starched beige security shirt, khaki tactical pants, and an eight-point duty cap.

"Don't make no quick movements, Mister," the man said in a John Wayne drawl. His other hand clutched at something on his right hip, presumably a gun. "Cops been looking for a truck like yours. Now where's the other one?"

"Other one?" Simon realized the guard was talking about Tel-Ba but how was he supposed to explain a talking column of blue smoke?

"This ain't no time to be a smartass. All I gots to do is pull out my cell phone and give the cops your license plate. Now, if you think you can outrun the Staties go right ahead, but I'll be damned if I let you out of this parking lot." On tiptoes, he was trying to see inside the cab of the truck.

"You want to see what's in the cab? Have a look." Simon pulled on the door handle until it clicked. Through the half open window, he heard another click, this one clean and crisp. He froze.

"Keep...the door...closed," the man said through clenched teeth. Feet shoulder width apart with arms outstretched to create a triangle between them, he pointed a huge revolver at Simon.

Simon inched his hands up in full view of the man's sightline. "Whoa there, buddy. Don't go pulling that trigger just yet. My daughter's in the passenger seat. I don't want her to get shot because of me."

"I heard three voices," the man said raising his volume. Beads of sweat formed on his forehead, making his skin sparkle. "Where's the other person?"

"Is this guy for real?" Hattie asked more relaxed than she should've been. She grabbed her dad's shoulder and used it to pull herself toward the half-open window. "Are you for real?"

"That's not helping, Hattie. Sit down." Simon tried to push her back to her side of the cab, but she kept finding ways around his hands.

"Our house just got an owl enema 'cause they think Cambion are evil." Pointing to the guard, she pulled her upper lip into a sneer. "Maybe if we tell him the whole story and show him Tel-ba, it'll scare him into letting us go."

Simon stared at his daughter.

Hattie's face looked murderous, as though she'd descended to a state of animalistic rage, but as soon as the look appeared, it faded, her green eyes becoming serene and calm.

"We aren't going to scare him into letting us go, Hattie."

"Ugh," said Hattie, throwing herself back to her seat. "Fine. I'm just a stupid girl."

"The man's got a gun pointed at us, Hattie."

"You two done arguing?" The guard inched his way forward, one hand gripped his revolver while his other hand pulled a flip-phone from a breast pocket. "I'm 'bout to call the police and let them settle this. I ain't got no time for people who won't cooperate." Trying to accomplish both tasks at once challenged his dexterity. The barrel of the revolver dipped as his fat fingers fumbled with the phone.

Something needed to happen if Simon was going to get them out of this. Then he realized how pale the man's face looked. He was a big boy, but the fear and dread in his face were uncharacteristic for a routine security check. Now, those bovine eyes weren't as unreadable as Simon first thought. Coupled with the man's lack of physical coordination, it was amazing Simon hadn't noticed sooner.

"Look, I don't know what's got you so panicked, but if you let me explain—"

The guard cut Simon off, "Yer not explaining anything till the cops are here, Mister."

"I just want to know why you're calling the cops in the first place. That's it."

The man thought about it, gun in one hand, and cell phone in the other. He was at it so long Simon heard Hattie hum the *Jeopardy* tune. The engine turned with a steady clink and clatter, begging for oil. A light in the parking lot flickered. Springs in the seat squeaked as Hattie adjusted her position, and, Simon noticed for the first time that Tel-ba was still in the breeze.

"No," the man said, retraining the gun on its target. "If you're that curious, you can ask your lawyer."

The guard held the phone up to dial, but Simon found he didn't much care.

An owl landed near the entrance of the parking lot. Light from the Comfort Inn sign illuminated its chocolate colored feathers. As the guard dialed, the owl hopped in his direction, moving with zigzag bursts, curious but unafraid.

Before realizing what he was doing, Simon flung the door open and moved toward the guard, pointing with an exaggerated overhand motion.

Flustered and panicked, the guard tossed the phone to the pavement, widened his stance and aimed. Hesitating, his shoulders slumped, and the gun lowered. Confusion rippled his chubby face.

Dashing across three parking spots, Simon grabbed the man and spun him around to face the owl. "That's one of the owls that attacked us. And believe me, if there's one here now it won't be long before this whole place is crawling with them."

The guard watched the bird hop within twenty feet of them. Comprehending no immediate danger, he shrugged off Simon's hand and stepped back. "Are you serious? That's what you're so jumpy about, an owl?"

"You don't get it…"

The guard pushed Simon back to the open door of the truck.

"Freaking weirdo," the guard said bringing the gun up again. "Get back in the vehicle before I blow your head off."

Simon's hands rose. Choosing to keep his mouth shut, he backed toward the truck. He wanted to rip the gun away from the man, but he knew that chance had come and gone. The guard's once docile eyes looked angry and confident.

The owl danced closer, it talons ticking against the pavement.

"Move it," the guard yelled matching Simon's steps.

Out of the corner of his eye Simon noticed a light come on in one of the second floor windows.

With a huge plume of brown and black feathers, the owl opened its beak as the hop transformed into a run, its head lowering with every stride.

"Would you listen for a minute?" Simon pleaded.

"NO. I'm done listening, Mister. I need *you* to get back in your truck."

Closing the distance, the owl stretched its neck and bit into the man's calf, ripping flesh and fabric from his leg.

"AHHHERRR. Stupid damn bird. What in the Hell is wrong with you?" The guard spun, kicked at his attacker. He missed, stumbled, and kicked again.

Wings flapped, feathers pitched into the air. The owl hopped back and forth as it hissed and hooted.

From where Simon stood he could see a ribbon of blood coating the guard's exposed leg, staining cloth and dripping onto the pavement. His own calf ached at the sight.

Behind them, Hattie yelled.

Simon looked around, found his daughter hanging out of the truck and pointing to a light pole near the building. On top of the pole, a barn owl spread its wings and swooped toward them.

Simon screamed to take cover.

The guard ducked, protecting his head with his forearms, as a barn owl swooped overhead and knocked off his duty cap.

The first owl moved in and snipped at the back of the guard's right ankle.

It may have been his imagination, but to Simon, the guard's Achilles tendon made a sound between a twang and a pop. A gruesome and chilling sound that made Simon's body wince with terror.

The guard howled. His leg twisted then buckled underneath him. Toppling backward, he scooted toward the building, right foot dragging on the ground. Chin-udders bouncing and spittle arcing from his lips, he aimed the gun at the chocolate colored fury.

The shot rang out, echoing through the Wyoming air. The owl turned into a cloud of fluff, red mist, and raw guts.

Simon started toward the guard but the man waved him back.

On the second floor, curtains rustled and split, a figure appeared in the light. How long before the police arrived?

The barn owl circled and landed on the back of the truck to Simon's left. It perched and rocked from side-to-side, hissing like a high pressure leak.

"AHHHH." Trembling with rage, the guard aimed at the owl on the bed of the truck. "NO." Simon screamed. The guard's firearm spoke for a second time, its death sentence ricocheting off the hotel in waves. Almost simultaneously the back window of the truck exploded in pebble-sized chunks. From somewhere a long way off Hattie screamed.

A plague of owls dropped from the darkness like huge raindrops. Owls landed everywhere, some big, some small, and they kept coming.

"HATTIE." Simon turned and ran for his daughter so hard it felt like his heart was in a wrestling match with his lungs. If she was hurt, he'd never forgive himself.

Half a dozen yellow-eyed owls were already on the truck, their talons ticking and scraping against metal as they perched and re-perched, flapping toward the disabled guard. Dozens more were on the ground, hissing and arching their wings, challenging each other for a better position on their prey.

Reaching the open door of the truck, Simon looked inside. The bench seat was empty. "HATTIE."

"I'm right here." She stuck an arm up from the floorboard. "That moron almost shot me"

"Stay there." Simon looked back to the guard. The poor bastard was fending off owls as best as he could, but it wasn't enough.

"You unholy rats with wings, DIE." The guard was shooting at anything with wings, emptying the revolver.

Each shot turned another owl inside out.

Seeking cover, Simon jumped in the truck.

The door panel Simon had been standing in front of jumped and produced a metallic *twang* as a couple bullets pierced sheet metal.

"DAD," Hattie screamed pulling her elbow up on the seat and leaning forward.

"Stay as far down as you can." Simon poked his head out to make sure it was safe to shut the door.

The guard, once proud, looked disheveled and powerless. He was using his revolver as a club, fighting the owls as they crowded around him. "Freaking birds…wings…kill you…" His quagmire of slurs and incoherencies filled the air. Streaks of blood ran down his arms and onto the concrete. Fear painted his face with a nervous expression that twitched back and forth between attackers. More owls joined in, using their talons to tear and dig into warm flesh. Worst of all, his eyes pleaded for help the same way drowning children plead for rescue.

To Simon's horror, a brown blur flew through the air and attached itself to the guard's head, drawing blood and fluttering for balance. The guard swung at the bird but its beak was quicker. The owl grabbed a finger and snapped it off like a twig. Blood poured from the stump. Then the bird bowed its head and dug its beak into the guard's right eye.

Fighting a wave of revulsion, Simon pulled the door shut and jammed the truck in reverse. He tried to ignore the screams, and anxious looks Hattie gave him, but he wasn't successful. As the truck rolled back, he could see the owls cover the guard's body. The feast had begun.

Simon shoved the gearshift into drive and stepped on the gas pedal. He didn't want to be around when the screams stopped. They were lucky to have made it this far.

Chapter 7

Turning north onto I-25, midnight traffic was non-existent. Simon slammed the gas pedal to the floorboard. The truck revved, caught traction, and sped up. He wanted out of this nightmare. All he could see was the guard's face as blood spilled across his tormented features. It wouldn't leave his thoughts.

"You can take it easy now, Dad."

"Come on, faster," Simon urged the truck. He knew what had happened was impossible. Owls don't travel in parliaments, not like that. And they sure as Hell don't attack humans unless they're provoked.

"Slow down."

Something touched his arm, and he jumped, jerking the wheel enough to send the tires skidding for a second. He corrected, gained control, and let the truck slow down under its own weight.

"Mom's right. You're nuts behind the wheel," Hattie said, punching Simon on the bicep.

He flinched and looked around until he met his daughter's eyes. Under a nest of black tangles, she looked more pissed than scared.

"Why are you hitting me?" Simon asked as the truck slowed to forty. He realized his hands shook. Thumb and pinkie bounced off the steering wheel, turning the beat into a double-time snare roll. He gripped the wheel to control himself.

"Where're we going?" Hattie asked as she covered her hand with her right sleeve and brushed glass off the seat.

"To your grandparents," he answered as he studied the rearview mirror. The blood on his forehead had dried to a crust and was flaking away.

"You can't do that." She stopped brushing glass and glared at him. "We have a responsibility."

"What responsibility, Hattie? We need help." He shook his head, clearing his thoughts a little. "You think this is a game. That guard back there is dead probably because of us."

"But Tel-ba…"

"Tel-ba isn't here." Simon yelled.

"You shouldn't give up on me so easily, human." Tel-ba hadn't reformed, but there was enough of him around to produce a voice.

"See," Hattie's eyes lit up with hopeful excitement as she looked around the cab. "Now we have to take him back."

"We don't have to do anything." Simon slammed his hand on the steering wheel. He wanted to grab the little blue spook around the throat and do the owl's job for them. Hattie flinched with each dash-rattling smack.

"You're the ones who put me together. You have to return me to my sanctuary." Blue smoke floated up from the seat of the truck like a flat blanket of fog.

"And why can't you just float back to the woods? You're a ghost, aren't you?" Simon asked.

In the headlights, a sign for Reservoir 3 told them the recreation area was a quarter mile ahead. That gave Simon a little time to figure out what he was doing.

"My spirit will only find entry to the Cambion sanctuary if my guide is with me." The smoke floating up from the seat swirled to a point next to Hattie's legs. Once his form had coalesced into a familiar column of bluish smoke, his image flickered back into existence.

Hattie's eyes turned into slits, her mood flipped like a light switch. "You don't know what they've been through. Tel-ba's shown me the blood that's been spilled. The owls don't kill for food. They kill for their own sick pleasure. The Cambion want to live in peace. What you should really ask is why the owl had a sudden urge to crash through our back door and chase us down like we were lunch. Or why it sent its stupid friends after us at the hotel."

176

The corner of Tel-ba's lips curled into a grin. "She has a point," he said as he hopped up on Hattie's lap and folded his arms across his chest.

"This isn't our fight," said Simon as his fingers gripped the steering wheel tighter, turning his knuckles white. He didn't like what was going on here. Hattie was impatient, opinionated, and passionate in her interests, but this fierce drive to help this ghost was beyond anything he'd ever witnessed from his daughter.

"You told me to be myself and never apologize for who I am," Hattie said. Her voice was firm and full of courage. "And twenty years from now I don't want to look back on this and regret not doing anything. We can help. We have to help."

"This is ridiculous." Simon shook his head in frustration and stared at the road, unwilling to see the resolve in his daughter's eyes.

"You always think you're Mr. Wisdom. Well, guess what? You aren't."

Simon turned onto the shoulder and slammed on the brakes, the wheels kicking up dirt and gravel, spraying the undercarriage as the rear axle locked up and slid to the right. Hattie braced herself, fearless as objects in the cab shifted to the front, rattling and bumping as inertia carried them.

"Knock that crap off, Hattie," he said as he shoved the gearshift into park and turned to his daughter. The guilt in his gut urged him to find the closest cop and explain everything from a holding cell. The only reason he'd come along this far was because he had no plan and no idea who to ask for help. According to Tel-ba, Hattie was the one with all the answers.

"Put the truck in drive. We're wasting time." Hattie's voice was steady, her nerve unyielding.

"Excuse me?" Simon couldn't believe what he was hearing.

"I'm doing what I think is right," she said. "Just because you're scared doesn't mean I am."

Simon paused and studied his daughter, thinking about what she was telling him. There were tears in her eyes, but they weren't just tears of sorrow. Mixed with a passionate resolve, they were tears of faith. And faith goes a long way. Not to mention, the evidence supported her ambitions. The owls had done nothing but torment, destroy, and kill. Tel-ba might be strange, but he was just trying to get home. He wondered why his anger toward the ghost had continued at all.

"Is that how it is then?" he asked. "You sure you want to use our earlier conversation as a basis for this argument?"

"It's not the argument I'm trying to win, Dad. I want your trust. If I don't have that, I've got nothing."

Simon rolled his eyes as his shoulders slumped in defeat. "Ugh, I can't believe I'm agreeing to this."

Hattie squealed with excitement, bouncing in her seat and repeating, "Thank You Thank You Thank You."

Simon felt his cheeks warm a little, and he couldn't help but smile. "Your mother's good at saying that kind of stuff too. Does the same damn thing to me all the time." As he pulled back onto the highway, he added, "Don't tell her I said that."

Ten minutes later, tires kicked up a cloud of dirt as Simon skidded onto Fish Creek Road and headed back into the mountains.

Chapter 8

Simon parked the Ford in the same spot they'd parked earlier. The overcast sky still refused to let starlight through, leaving the surrounding forest in a heavy blanket of shadows. Large swaths of darkness hid behind the trees and threw off Simon's depth perception as they mingled with one another in a weave of vertical lines.

He moved to get out, but Hattie grabbed his arm and pulled him back.

"Wait," she said leaning forward to study the tree-line.

"We must wait for our escort," added Tel-ba, completing Hattie's thought.

"An escort?" Simon asked. "Who's gonna escort us, more ghosts?"

"When you see them, you'll know what I mean," Tel-ba said as he drifted onto the dash and joined Hattie in her search. His focus switched from the woods to the sky and back again. He looked nervous.

Simon couldn't see anything. The low branches created an effective wall of indistinguishable shadows. It was like trying to see the center of a cornfield while scouting its perimeter. "How long do we have to wait?"

"Not long," Hattie said. She never even glanced in her father's direction. If anything, her intense focus on the pines increased, squeezing her eyes into a narrow glare.

"How do you..." Simon's words were lost, replaced by eerie wonder as the pines in front of them lit up like Christmas lights. The effect reminded Simon of fireflies, but he'd never seen them at this elevation. He realized the sparkles were paired, moving in exact synchronization with a mate. It was light reflecting off their eyes. And by the looks of things there were hundreds, and that was only where the headlights illuminated the trees.

Hattie turned to her father. "Now, we go."

They left the truck running with both doors wide open. Simon exited out of the driver's side and Hattie out of the passenger's with Tel-ba sitting securely in her cupped hands. The road was still wet from the rain, but the hard packed dirt remained firm. Making their way to the front of the truck, their small group waited in the Ford's headlights.

Across the small clearing, the Cambion spilled out of the pines in a mob. Their scrambling bodies crawled and jumped over one another, blanketing the area like a plague of furless rats. Pale gray skin and wild tuffs of hair, they looked similar to Tel-ba. Some were small while others were tall and thin. The group was as diverse as any crowd.

Yet, among the entire throng Simon saw no children.

The Cambion formed into two columns that reached halfway to the truck. The two lines faced each other like some kind of military ceremony. All they were missing, Simon decided, were little sabers to hoist over their heads.

"Quick, we must follow," Tel-ba said hopping from Hattie's hands. The little nightmare glided to the ground and made a dash down the path of Cambion. Moving in an eerie blue blur, the collection of smoke disappeared into the trees.

Hattie watched him go and stepped toward the open path. Simon reached out and stopped her, catching her shoulder and stretching her shirt as she strained for freedom.

"I—I can't. I gotta follow Tel-ba," Hattie said. "I have to."

"No you don't, Hattie."

"Tel-ba's shown me the path I must take. I can't ignore that." She stopped pulling and pushed instead, throwing off Simon's balance. Twisting her shoulders, she freed herself and followed Tel-ba into the foliage.

Simon tripped two steps backward and crashed to the ground. His head pinged off the Ford's bumper snapping his teeth together with a loud *clack*. His vision rattled in his eye sockets.

"Hattie, come back." The ringing pain between his ears stretched to the front of his skull like fingers.

Ten feet away the Cambion scrambled toward the trees. Simon heard little yips and yells as if they were excited about something.

"Hattie." He tried to get to his feet, but his head forced him back down with a wave of dizziness and a fresh spike of pain.

Trying to figure out what was going on Simon stretched his eyelids open and stared in dumbfounded revulsion. Was he seeing things? Could tonight get any worse? Dozens of owls swooped through the headlights picking up exposed Cambion like they were discarded popcorn. The owls used their hooked beaks to rip the heads off their victims before dropping the carcasses and diving in for more. Sprays of blood created a mist that hung in the air like a crimson fog.

Simon yelled trying not to focus on the surrounding carnage, but the sounds were too much to block out. The chorus of death pounded at his brain filling his skull with a cacophony that clouded his fatherly drive with complete effectiveness. Beaten back against the bumper, he huddled his knees to his chest, closed his eyes, and prayed for this macabre nightmare to end.

Chapter 9

After a while the devastating song of death died away, but he stayed where he was. His head rang. His body cried out from more than a dozen wounds. Hattie would be back. She had to come back.

With his eyes still closed, he felt a strong gust accompanied by the flapping sounds of many wings. He knew how the two sensations were related.

Simon opened his eyes and felt ice touch his spine. All around him, circling the nose of the Ford in crescent formation, the owls watched—every kind from pygmy owls that live as far south as Guatemala to the Great Gray Owl of the northern hemisphere. At their center was the Great Horned Owl that had followed them for most the night. It too watched him, shifting its head from side to side. Hunched in its awkward gait, it stepped forward and spread its wings wide enough to engulf the front of the truck.

Familiar browns and tans cupped Simon like the inside of a giant egg. Above him, the face of the giant Great Horned Owl loomed. Feathers around its eyes revolved as they had on his first encounter with the bird. The wings vibrated hypnotically. This time, however, he felt the pulsing those vibrations created. They bounced off his body in numbing waves, putting his nerves to sleep, paralyzing him. The air warbled against his eardrums, changing tempo, shifting through frequencies, soothing his consciousness into sleep. There was no escape.

As he slipped into unconsciousness, his sleep filled with images—Hattie running into the forest surrounded by little gray creatures, opening the owl pellet and finding the skull of Tel-ba, the owl's attack on the truck, the giant pellet in a plastic baggie.

"You have destroyed this world," a voice said. Its tone was powerful and old, ancient perhaps. "But since you are sacred to this planet, we will afford you a few faults."

"Sacred?"

"There is much humans don't know, and far more you will never understand."

"Who said we're sacred?"

"Aumakua," said the voice, "the ancient guardians of Man, but you fail to ask the right questions. Your daughter has escaped. Your way of life is threatened."

"What about my daughter?"

"She is Taken," said the voice. "And the Taken are possessed, bewitched into believing they are needed. On that need, the Cambion prey. And once your daughter is within their sanctuary, they will sacrifice her to bring back the one you call Tel-ba. They are the offspring of the incubi and succubi of the world, and they will go as far as they need to carry out their dark prophecies."

"You attacked my family. You destroyed my house. You killed that guard. Why should I believe anything you say?"

"Our duty is to protect. What happened to the guard was unfortunate."

"Unfortunate? That man was doing his job, and you killed him."

The voice thundered in the deepest recesses of Simon's mind. "I do not control all owls, human. I tried to warn you, and you didn't listen. Are you willing to make the same mistake twice?"

Chapter 10

When Simon opened his eyes, the owls were gone. The only trace left behind was a solitary feather on the ground at his feet. It was the verification he needed.

Using the truck for support, he rose to his feet and hesitated when the pressure in his head threatened to put him down again. He earned a concussion from hitting his head on the bumper, but he decided not to think about it until he got Hattie back.

He turned and gave the trees a hard look. He wondered if the owl could be right. If he was, that meant Hattie could be roasting over an open fire, or worse, eaten alive. The trees offered no advice.

Out of the darkness, Hattie's giggles drifted back to him. The sound made Simon's neck hairs stand at attention.

Her voice energized him, urging him to run into the forest in a blind fury. Instead, he turned his head to the sky. "Okay, I'm going after her, and I'm bringing her back."

Chapter 11

Simon's eyes adjusted to the murky space between trees, yet he navigated with slow caution. His head pounded, his body ached, but the sound of his daughter's voice kept him going. Partly crouched, he chose his steps as if hunting, avoiding twigs and leafy branches for fear of the noise. Every fourth step he paused to listen.

A good fifty yards from the truck, he came to some buckbrush on the edge of a clearing. The musky smelling from its tiny white flowers forced him to bury his nose in the crook of his elbow.

Simon risked looking around the brush. The clearing was forty feet wide, surrounded by Ponderosas and dying aspens. Rocks pushed through the barren topsoil in random clusters. At the opposite end, a crowd of Cambion covered more than a quarter of the clearing. Gathered around a fire, they cast shadows that danced and flickered across the ground, hiding Hattie's whereabouts.

Simon crouched low and flanked to the left. As he got closer, he could hear them chanting, huffing, and grunting with a practiced rhythm. The sound reminded him of horror movies where tribal ceremonies lead to cannibalistic table manners.

With less than twenty feet between him and the crowd, he ducked behind a Ponderosa and watched the Cambion dance in a state of worship. Their focus centered on the tree line, putting Simon at the crowd's back. From where he squatted, he saw hundreds of the hellish creatures. Using their knees like springs, they launched themselves skyward in eerie unison. In midair, they shot out their arms before plummeting back to the ground and starting over.

Gripping the thick, vanilla scented tree bark, Simon straightened his legs and stood for a better view. At first all he saw was a crowd of little gray bodies dancing around a fire. As he let his eyes readjust to the firelight, he noticed a makeshift stage at the base of a tree, the focal point of their worship. Little more than a flat piece of wood stacked on a pile of rocks, there was plenty of room for the two Cambion who stood above the rest. The one wearing the strange headdress made of bones looked old and impatient. A scowl seemed permanently etched into his face. The one to his left faded in and out of focus as if the fog that made up his body grew restless.

"Tel-ba," Simon said under his breath.

Sitting next to the stage with her legs stretched out in front of her, Hattie grinned and watched the crowd with curious eyes.

Simon's heart did backflips. He almost broke cover to yell her name, but that meant announcing his presence.

The Cambion in the bone headdress walked forward and raised his hands. The board beneath him creaked as if under a tremendous weight. At the gesture, the crowd turned silent, watchful.

"Eons ago, in days long forgotten by mortal man, we were born out of sin between demons and humans. Their fornications did not stand trial. Instead, the world abhorred our birth and hunted us down. *Hell Spawn* they called us, yet we were the victims. Since then we have suffered long, my fellow Cambion. True, humans have forgotten, but the owls carry on their duties for them. Do we deserve this? Did we ask for this? Did we ask to be born to a life of fear?"

"NO," cried the listeners, their hysteria emphasized with three thumps to the chest and more jumping.

"The truth is spoken." The one wearing the headdress spoke louder and louder. He was rallying them together. "We only want to exist and live peaceful lives. Humanity owns the planet, so why do we get the damp nightmare that keeps us hiding? Because we are doomed to extinction? I, Larr-tuk, Giver of tribe Cam-baa, will not let that end befall us. We have our sacrifice. With her, we will see the safety of immortality."

Beating their chests again, the mass-hysteria of the crowd grew into a cheer of triumph. Some of them yelled so loud and beat so hard, they looked like rabid dogs, foaming at the mouth.

Above the raucousness, Hattie screamed.

Simon stepped from cover, terrified of what he would see. "Hattie!"

"Dad?" Her voice echoed surprise, not fear.

Where was she? Simon couldn't see her around the glare of the fire. She sat next to the stage a second ago, but now he was unable to follow the sound of her voice, and he was in the open.

A slow domino effect rippled through the Cambion, fanning out until they all stared at Simon. Their eyes were black peas polished to a high gleam.

Simon's body heated up. Adrenalin became his tool for motivation. He knew there was no way out of this. It was fight or flight. Leaving his daughter behind wasn't an option.

"Take him," said Larr-tuk, pointing at Simon with an authoritative finger.

Yelling with every inch of lung he had, Simon charged toward the crowd. Achieving a full sprint, he kicked a boney looking Cambion, anticipating the gratifying crunch.

Instead, his foot ignited with pain as the Cambion caught his boot and stopped him in his tracks. Every bone in his foot felt shattered. The nerve endings screamed. He tumbled forward in a long arch. His face slammed against the ground. The fall knocked the air out of him.

Simon flipped over, gasping, latching on to shock and adrenaline. He tried to get back on his feet, but the pain was too much and forced him back to the ground. They swarmed him, their bodies felt like small cannonballs pelting him through his clothes. The weight bore him down and pinned his torso with so much force that the pain in his foot became secondary.

"Hattie," Simon gasped.

"Do you see what comes before us, brothers and sisters?" asked Larr-tuk, a shepherd leading his flock. "Do you see what has come into our lives with rage and hatred? What did we do to him?"

"Nothing," the crowd droned.

"Sounds like B.S. to me," Simon said weak and desperate. With the weight of the combined Cambion sitting on him, each breath was earned through exertion.

"To you it would sound that way," said Tel-ba. "Turn his head so he can see."

Dozens of creepy ghoulish hands gripped Simon's hair and turned his head toward the fire and the stage set up ten feet away on his left. Larr-tuk held a knife and stood next to a ceremonial chalice the size of a thimble. Tel-ba stood behind him, and Hattie, as if waiting for a corsage from a prom date, offered her wrist above the chalice.

"Witness our salvation." The Cambion leader held the knife aloft, ready to strike.

"Nooo. Leave her alone," Simon wheezed as he struggled under the weight of the creatures. He had to save her but the more he fought for freedom the less strength he had.

Then, without cue or warning, Larr-tuk pierced Hattie's wrist. His stab was quick and precise.

Refusing to pull away, she inhaled sharply, biting her lower lip to stifle a groan.

Blood dripped into the chalice.

The crowd howled with ecstasy, but the group on Simon's chest remained silent, aware of their duties.

Once the chalice was full Hattie pulled her wrist back and nursed the cut. It didn't look serious. It wasn't what Simon expected. Didn't the owls say Cambion were bad? Shouldn't Hattie's wrist be pouring blood?

"Now drink, Tel-ba! Drink and find solidity in this world once more. Rise from the dust of your bones and end our suffering."

Tel-ba focused on the blood as he cupped his hands and dipped them into the chalice. He brought them back up and drank. Red streaks dribbled down his chin and onto his chest.

His body's reaction was gradual, using every bit of the fluid. First, the mist swirled in on itself, forming the bones Simon and Hattie pulled from the owl pellet. The process continued up to his shoulders where it spread like wildfire. Second by second, his body re-formed using blood to revitalize his existence until he was the same dingy gray as the rest of his kind.

Finally, Tel-ba was whole.

The crowd of Cambion chanted in a low, breathy cadence, holding their hands above their heads in reverential praise. Even Hattie appeared excited. She joined in the celebration, sticking two fingers in her mouth and whistling.

Tel-ba stepped to the edge of the stage. Lifting his emaciated arms into the air he calmed the crowd.

As the crowd quieted, Simon took the opportunity to interrupt. "Let us go, Tel-ba. You got what you wanted." His struggles became more ferocious, desperate.

"I do have what I wanted." Tel-ba gazed over at Simon. "But I don't have what the prophecy promised us. Your daughter will do that."

Letting anger fuel him, Simon struggled against his captors. His right arm slipped free. He grabbed one of the Cambion standing on his chest. He was victorious. He would get out of this. It was like clutching a cold stone fresh from the earth. Simon flexed, tried to move the creature, but it wouldn't budge. Obsidian eyes glared down. Against all hope, rumbling laughter pulsed in Simon's grip.

Another wave of Cambion hurried over to help restrain their captive.

Small fingers pinched as they re-pinned Simon's arm. Others pulled at his clothes, stretching the fabric until threads popped.

"She has nothing you want," Simon cried, fighting for air again. His vision blurred. He had to save Hattie. He'd tried everything. Nothing worked. He'd failed.

Hattie stood and walked toward her father, Cambion spreading to make a path for her. "It's okay, Dad." She tilted her head to one side and pulled her eyebrows together in a look of concerned bemusement. "Tel-ba promised no one will get hurt." Her eyes traveled over the cuts before working their way down to Simon's crumpled foot. The boot was at an odd angle and refused to budge. "Well, no one else anyway."

"This is crazy, Hattie," said Simon, pleading. His own voice wavered under the weight of his physical and emotional pains. He pressed on, shoving words out of his mouth with increasing effort. "We need to get out of here and to a hospital."

"Not yet." She knelt beside him and touched his face with a gentle hand, wiping away tears.

"What else do they want, Hattie?" He stared into her eyes searching for rationality. It wasn't there. "Tel-ba got what he wanted, why won't you help me get what I want?"

"Dad, you know I can't," she sounded as if Simon still had a choice. "I have to help Tel-ba and the others."

"I want to go home, Hattie." He cried, sobbing between short sniffles. "I want both of us to go home."

Hattie leaned down and kissed her father's forehead. "And we will, I promise," she whispered. "After we're done here, we'll get all the help we need." She stood and made her way back to the stage.

"Hattie, don't go. Hattie. Hattie."

She didn't listen; she was lost, she was…Taken.

"Join with me and praise the dawning of a new era," said Larr-tuk.

The crowd dropped to their knees and bowed in a steady rhythm. They responded with fervent moans. "Mmmmuh-da, Mmmmuh-da, Mmmmuh-da." Even the Cambion holding Simon down, though not free to bow, moaned at this penultimate moment.

Hattie lay down in front of the stage and positioned her head at its center.

"With these two vessels we have been granted the salvation of a new life," continued Larr-tuk.

Tel-ba stepped to the edge of the stage and knelt in front of Hattie's face. It looked like he joined the rest of the Cambion, bowing and praying to whatever god they worshipped. But then, shoving his hands into Hattie's mouth, he pulled her lips apart and slid inside. He wriggled and squirmed working his way deeper and deeper into her throat.

Hattie's eyes went wide as her airway was cut off, but she didn't spit or pull Tel-ba out. Instead, as his shoulders disappeared behind her lips she arched her back and opened her mouth wider.

"Hattie!" Simon yelled. There was nothing he could do but watch Tel-ba disappear inside his daughter's mouth.

Her eyes rolled. She twitched and squirmed, articulating anguish with every motion. After what seemed like a lifetime, Tel-ba's legs and feet slipped out of view and the convulsions stopped.

Watching the nightmare images of Hattie's death, knowing Hattie was dead, Simon struggled against the Cambion, thrusting against their weight in desperate turns and twists. *I need my daughter. I need to make sure she's okay. She's so smart. She has the world before her. She can't die. Not here.*

"I'll kill you." Simon peered around at the Cambion. "I'm gonna come back and burn these woods to the ground. Whoever's left, I'm gonna trap and feed to the damn owls. You hear me you little rodents? I'm gonna crush your bones to dust."

Larr-tuk laughed, filling the clearing with an eerie sound that echoed off the trees. He walked from the stage and climbed onto Simon's chest. He seemed much older than Tel-ba. The lines in his face made him appear part lizard, and the pitch black orbs of his eyes gave a demented look.

"You may go but when you do come back, it will not be to kill us. When you come back, you will bring us your other children and your wife. When you come back our numbers will grow."

"Stick that head of yours in my mouth and I'll bite it off," said Simon.

Larr-tuk laughed again while he removed his headdress and handed it to one of his entourage. The subservient creature accepted the crown and disappeared into the crowd. "You don't get it, human. You've lost. You've lost your daughter. And now, you will lose your body."

"Relax, Dad," Hattie said as she moved into view. "We're doing a good thing here."

She looked unharmed. Even the pale sheet of death that colored her face only a moment ago was gone.

"Hattie? Are you okay?" Her eyes told him she was far from okay. Once hazel with flecks of gold around her pupils, the irises had darkened to match those of a Cambion. Hattie was gone.

Tiny fingers pulled his lips apart, grabbing his skin like pincers, and yanking facial hair. They pulled at his teeth, forcing his jaw open. He tried to bite down, but the force snapped both upper incisors at the gum line with a *crack*. Pain seared through his head, drenching his face in magma and forcing Simon's mouth open, a scream tried to issue from his throat.

The scream was cut off as Larr-tuk dove in.

Simon felt the long emaciated Cambion arms slide across his tongue and past his uvula, bringing with them a revolting taste. He gagged, but the more he tried to dislodge the Cambion the less effect it had. He would die of asphyxiation, and, just like his daughter, his body would lure more victims to their death.

In the last moment, Simon's chest tightened and the edge of his vision shrank, making room for a universal numbness to take over his senses. He focused on his daughter one last time, closed his eyes, and…

AUTHOR BIOGRAPHIES

ANTHONY BARTLEY has been fascinated by creepy things lurking in the dark since he was a three-year-old boy listening to his grandmother tell tales of monsters and ghosts. With that grotesque seed planted so long ago, he went on to be published in small press horror magazines (Macabre and The Murder Hole), anthologies (Kings of the Night and Hauntings) and webzines (Alien Skin, Dark Krypt, and The Harrow), as well as Perspective(s)—San Juan College's annual literary magazine. He recently finished his first young adult novel, Freak Show Summer, about a 1930s carnival freak show. Currently, he is working on the first novel in the series called Kids Investigating the Paranormal (KIP). Follow him on twitter: @TonyinNM.

E. CLUFF ELLIOTT (aka. The Farmington Scribbler) was born and raised in Farmington, New Mexico, where he lives with his beautiful wife and two perfect daughters. In his youth, English was his worst class. The irony of becoming a horror author has not escaped him. Writing for more than ten years, he has several short stories published online, including one story that appears in the anthology Bonded by Blood V: Doomsday Descends. He also earned an Honorable Mention in the 78th Writer's Digest Annual Competition. If you're curious about Cluff's current projects please email him at: e_cluff13@yahoo.com.

LINDA FREDERICKS moved to the Rocky Mountain region of Wyoming after graduating from college. A career educator she taught at the elementary, secondary and post secondary levels in Wyoming and New Mexico. She writes fiction, non-fiction and poetry and has had a number of short stories, flash fiction and poems published in literary journals including Red Mesa Review (University of New Mexico). Currently, she is working on her first novel, My Australia, a chapbook project entitled Capturing the Essence, and Long Story, Shorts: A Bio-mythography. You may email her at: ohen49@yahoo.com.

TRACI HALESVASS wrote a poem when she was seven, to great familial reviews. She received so much exuberant expression she got it in her head she was meant to be a writer. Thus, she subjected her life to the calling. She received a masters and a MFA in creative writing. Recently, she retired from a professorship in teaching writing. Her publications include short stories, flash fiction, and poems in literary journals and newspapers across the country. She is on the final revision of her first novel and working on a second. In her retirement she hosts a local radio program interviewing other authors. You may email her at: halesvasst@sanjuancollege.edu.

GLORIA O'SHIELDS is an award-winning writer with published works in fiction, nonfiction, and poetry. Her lighthearted novel, Quinn's Quest, has received honors in national book competitions. She is also the co-author of We Shall Be Heard: Women Speakers in America, a scholarly collection of speeches with biographical and rhetorical commentary. Always intrigued by the unexplained, she is currently writing a mystery. A graduate of the University of Southern California she is a retired educator and lives in New Mexico. She is a founding member of San Juan Writers. Visit her website at: gloriaoshields.com.

LEE PIERCE writes traditional western fiction reminiscent of the westerns of the 1950's and 60's. His novels feature solid plots, strong multifaceted characters, and plenty of action. He has five novels published, with number six due out soon. He is a founding member of San Juan Writers and a member of Western Fictioneers. A former restaurateur, Pierce is the author of a successful cookbook, What Do You Mean the Cook's Not Mexican? He is a veteran of numerous book signings around the Southwest and lives in Farmington, New Mexico with his lovely wife, Cathy. You can find his books on: Amazon.com and Kindle.

VICKY RAMAKKA was published in academic journals, wrote grant applications, reports, and a variety of marketing materials during her academic career. Since retiring from San Juan College, she enjoys the freedom to write creatively. Ramakka has published articles in local, regional and national magazines. Her articles have won New Mexico Press Women awards for personality profiles and feature magazine stories. Her first mystery novel, The Cactus Plot, is available from Artemesia Publishing. See more of Vicky's stories and photos at her website: vrwriting.wordpress.com.

ROBERTA SUMMERS is an award-winning author with a creative writing degree from San Juan College in Farmington, New Mexico. She is published in poetry and short stories and is the author of two novels. Pele's Realm, a crime/adventure set on Hawaii's Big Island, and Fatal Winds, a fact based story about Downwinders and nuclear pollution are both currently available on Amazon.com. The former co-owner of Silverjack Publishing, she has also served as editor for Perspective(s): Art and Literary Magazine. About her writing, she says, "I write because I have something to say, and I want to be heard—it's a burning desire." Visit her website: robertasummers.com, or follow her on Facebook.

Made in the USA
Columbia, SC
06 September 2021